Salsa

JENNIFER LYNCH

ABOUT THE AUTHOR

Jennifer is a very keen dancer. She has danced since the age of sixteen. She started salsa around twenty years ago. If you ask her, what she loves best, she would no doubt say being with her pets, springer spaniel Barney and ginger tom Sunny. Following that there's a close tie between writing and dancing which she's combined in this book. Jennifer has been writing for many years whilst enjoying her life in the Suffolk Countryside. As well as this book, she has written: -

The Silver Lining
Never to be Told
William's Wishes
Liberty Angel
We Hear You Angels
Shades of Kefalonia

Attracting What you Really Want (ebook)
She is a radio host for the Natural Co-Creators Show on Blog Talk Radio, also on YouTube. You will find her at Mind Body & Soul events giving Angel Card Readings along with Empowerment Coaching. She is also a trained, holistic therapist.

Contact her at www.angelwisdom.co.uk

Published by Jennifer Lynch
www.angelwisdom.co.uk

ISBN: 978-1-5272-9060-0

DEDICATION

To the dancers unable to dance – we'll return strengthened!

And to my dear friend Stefan who gave me this fantastic review SHINE ON!

SALSA – a novel by Jennifer Lynch

Who could resist that title? The characters drew me in right away.

A fascinating inside view of the internal conflicts, insecurities and compulsions.

The steamy bits are all the better for the realism

- hot and urgent while driven by deeper desires which may remain unmet. The contrast between the female and male perspective is well drawn.

Each character justifies their impulsive actions to themselves, and this adds the knowing complicity between author and reader.

A gripping story with 'behind the scenes' insights about the Salsa scene. I couldn't stop myself from compulsively reading on!

Stefan Freedman

Author and Salsa teacher

Miranda Campbell (Anglia Salsa)

Your teaching has been a joy – fun, exciting and always entertaining.

To Judith Atkins – Salsa Dancer and Salsa Teacher thank you for your patience and excellent feedback.

CHAPTER 1
RETAIL THERAPY – LINDA

Linda's phone vibrated in her pocket. She knew it was only a text, but she found it annoying when browsing in her favourite shop. The message was from Cameron. What does he want, she wondered with a heavy heart? Linda thought it safer not to look than to risk becoming upset and quickly wiped a tear from her face. Five that ought to be enough, she muttered as she forced herself to focus on the pile in front of her. Since giving up her meds, talking to herself had become a habit. She had stopped taking her tablets weeks ago because they made her dizzy. When dancing came first falling over on the dance floor wasn't an option!

The salsa and soul weekender in the south of France was fast approaching, and it was going to be hot. Linda was more comfortable in long floaty dresses than bespoke dance clothes, and she'd selected some fabulous garments in bright, cheerful colours which were perfect for the dance weekend. Speaking French could be a problem because she hadn't spoken it for years. Her honeymoon in France was now a distant memory. It was a different stage in her life when she was young and in love, how times had changed. She was entirely different.

Her thoughts drifted to her husband, Adrian. She was surprised he hadn't objected to this trip, but then she'd told him the group consisted of her female friends. Over the last few years, white lying had become a natural way forward. If she let her hair down too frequently, Adrian made her feel guilty. It was apparent that her husband had no intention of joining her at any of her dance classes, so his complaints were futile. He sometimes appeared resentful, but he was unprepared to change when he seldom looked up from his laptop!

Linda tried on the first dress and began to feel excited about the trip. She had a beautiful slim figure which Adrian described as petite. Her appearance brought her compliments, but she was unhappy with her body because her breasts were small in comparison to others, plus bras that plunged were uncomfortably irritating.

When Linda danced, her body twisted and swayed in a hypnotic motion which caused envy among her dance friends. Linda was unaware of her beauty preferring to see herself as skinny and flat-chested. She lacked self-love. She picked up the pile of the dresses then quickly put one back on the rail. It was too formal. It reminded her of dinners when her drinking had been out of control, but God, honestly, Adrian's work colleagues were so dull. She sighed deeply, why care if the dress went back on the rail correctly, no-one would buy it!

Linda quickly headed to the counter to pay. Surprisingly they totalled £356. Wow, her bill was usually double that. The sales were fantastic. Her phone buzzed again, and another text appeared, so she made her way to the café on the next floor to take a breather. She was lucky to find a little table in what seemed a quiet corner. She then sat down, took a few long deep breaths and opened Cameron's message. 'What?' she thought, feeling perplexed and started to re-read it.

'Hi Linda, are you free tonight? I can come over at 8? x.'

Why did he act as if nothing had happened, when over the last few weeks, she'd been on a roller coaster? She couldn't believe Cameron had so little regard for her feelings. He treated their relationship like a game.

The tea was welcome, and Linda relaxed slightly and put her phone on the café table. She suddenly noticed her scone had appeared, but she hadn't seen the waitress. It was delicious. Linda didn't know how to respond to Cameron's message, but she once again recalled the words he said when they last met. 'You do realise this will be our last night together, don't you?' So why did he say that? Perhaps he enjoyed the drama of leaving her tied in knots. Couldn't he see that she was a woman with feelings? But if she ended it, what would she do? It was impossible to return to Adrian's lovemaking. For one, she didn't want to try and two she couldn't force herself to rekindle their passion when the memory of him jumping on top of her, made her shudder! She couldn't think of the last time they showed each other affection. Her menopause had been the perfect opportunity to declare their sex life over. At least she wouldn't have to fake an orgasm or see Adrian's face leering down at her. She quickly took a sip of tea, hoping the caffeine would bring her to her senses. It was better not to worry about resurrecting things when Adrian accepted her excuses. He was unaware that a few months later, she was enjoying sex with her new lover! Linda discovered that appreciation worked wonders for combatting Adrian's moodiness. Handling him was a skill. She had no doubt her husband was a great provider, but thirty years was a long time, and they'd both changed. His business trips were convenient because she wanted to spend time dancing and with Cameron. Fortunately, Adrian enjoyed his time away, which was a blessing, and his text messages weren't too intrusive!

The salsa class had been a miracle for Linda. Her only regret was she hadn't learned to dance years ago but better late than never, and she intended to make the best of it. After discovering an advertisement in her local paper, Linda joined the beginner's class at Club Cubanica, then religiously turned up every Thursday evening for the next six months, after discovering she was rather good at it! What also excited her was there were plenty of men to dance with, so she was never short of partners. Fortunately, everyone was friendly, and the dancers swopped continuously, which meant they all learned quickly. Linda became slimmer, fitter and happier. Dancing had improved her confidence, and in her fifties, she began to experience some excitement!

Adrian noticed how happy his wife was, but he wasn't interested in learning to dance. In the early days, she asked him to join her, but he could never make the time, so he reluctantly allowed her to get on with it! Since then, Linda had never looked back, and salsa was now a big part of her life. So why take a husband? Adrian would curtail her, and she didn't need unnecessary baggage!

Over the last few weeks, her spending habits had escalated. Today was Wednesday which consisted of a trip into town for dance dresses and browsing around the book stores for erotic novels. Linda had already been through the ones the library stocked, which had been better for her purse, but sadly they didn't stock many! She could download books to her kindle for free, but browsing gave her the excuse to go into town, which filled her time. Staying at home was at times a little dull with only their dog Peanut for company!

Linda's feelings of loneliness had escalated over the past two years since Ian left for University, and Fiona left for Japan. It felt as if her children were a million miles away, and she missed them. Her friends often referred to it as empty nest syndrome, but it was more than that, her emotions were raw because no one listened.

Her mind drifted to Cameron's breath on the back of her neck and the weight of his body on hers. Their rhymical movements had quickly led to a state of ecstasy. Did he say it was the last time they would be together or had she imagined it? The tears she'd shed, but part of her knew it wasn't over. He said she was the best lover he'd ever had, so why would he go? They never discussed the future, but what did that matter when they had an incredible connection? Adrian was safe and secure, but she had decided a long time ago he wasn't her 'forever man.' Their kisses had gone, and she'd recently taken to offering her cheek as a greeting. Her husband worked hard to bring in the bread which she carved up and spread with jam, but that was life! She had been a good wife for many years, so she didn't feel any shame in her withdrawal. It was natural that things would change as they grew older, and there was acceptance in that. Linda quickly checked her online banking which felt slightly odd in a café. Where on earth had her money gone? She had a small income from preparing the occasional wedding flowers, which Adrian reluctantly topped up with weekly payments. Still, she was surprised how fast her money disappeared!

Linda had been a full-time florist in her other life, before the children. She had been artistic and talented, which she had loved. It was sad that her talents had never developed enough to open a shop because the energy of flowers always uplifted her, and now she relied on a lover!

She continued to think about Cameron's skin glistening in the moonlight, as the light shone through her bedroom window. He always held her reassuringly, they felt like one, but they were very different. She was, educated, delicate and sophisticated, and Cameron was rough and at times far too blunt! But by some miracle, their energies blended along with their passion. Joy swept through her body, taking her to places she had never experienced, and she didn't want to return to her mundane life. She couldn't remember much about Cameron's home life, except that he worked in health and safety but did it matter, he was her lover and equal. She noticed things had changed over the past few weeks after the bliss subsided, there had been some awkward silences followed by Cameron repeating.

'You know we won't last, don't you? How can it? Will you leave Adrian for me? Give up what you have?' But she had closed her ears to it. Maybe he was right. Their love was of the moment, and she found it too painful to acknowledge. Her emotions were out of control due to the fear of them parting. And now Cameron was back, wanting to be with her tonight? Was it fair? What if Adrian arrived home early from his business trip and found them together, in their house! How would he react? Would he throw her out, or worse still tell the children! She was too old for this!

Adrian's text message said he was away on business for the next few days, but he hadn't specified the day he returned. He'd rarely phone; instead, she'd receive a text, saying 'I'm sorry Linda, but I won't be back tonight,' or 'I'm on my way,' but she couldn't rely on it. Seeing Cameron was easy to arrange, but emotionally, it was something else. She wanted to see him. They had a connection. Whether it was physical, past life, or lust, its flame was hard to extinguish. Despite this, she knew it would be her who severed their connection because there would be a time for not going back!

Linda sipped her tea and continued to think of Cameron. She imagined her hands exploring his muscles, his deep brown eyes piercing deeply into hers. She was hot and felt a bead of sweat trickle down her back into the top of her underwear, and she adjusted herself in her seat! The warmth of her body reminded her of the heat from Cameron's body as his eager tongue slid down her spine. She suddenly felt uncontrollably sexy and wanted to purchase new underwear, something that would entice him. She had to stop this because she was in a constant state of arousal, having no control over her sexual thoughts. Yet the other side of her wanted them to remain together. She finished her tea, then remembered that drinking caffeine was terrible for hot flushes! Oh well, she needed it right now. It was a shame it had been such a small cup!

Finding the energy to dance was sometimes exhausting and so was hiding her age. At least her Doctor had agreed to the HRT because it was cheaper than Botox and the other menopausal symptoms had disappeared. It was her secret, and it would stay that way because right now, growing old wasn't an option. Maybe in a few years when her love affairs were over, she would relax into it! She'd finished her tea and now needed to go home and plan which dress to wear. What could she cook for dinner? If Cameron didn't appear this evening, no doubt she'd see him at dancing this week, but that meant sharing him with others! Their passion was dependent on her secrecy, or their affair would be over. Linda sighed, picked up her shopping bags and headed towards the car park. Purchasing new underwear was no longer a priority when her bank balance was shockingly low, and she still had to find time to walk Peanut!

CHAPTER 2

ONE MOMENT PLEASE JADE

Jade fiddled with her shoes. The straps had cut into her heels and were causing her pain, and she regretted putting them on. They were high for work, but the style made her appear tall and slim. Her headset also irritated her because it kept sliding forward and she was now ready to throw it in the bin.

It was 4.30 p.m. on a Wednesday, in early June. Jade liked to leave work on the dot of 5, apart from the odd occasion when there was an urgent message. Jade loved her job as a receptionist at Tomlinson and Wilson but repeating herself had become wearing. She was happy that her sister was styling her hair next week, which would help with the headset issue which had been going on for weeks. Her sister was a hairdresser so they could do an exchange, hair for nails. Jade was good at nails. She loved creating new designs which always went down well with her sister. She hadn't had any formal training, but she was naturally creative, and her sister said they were stunning.

Jade was twenty-nine years old and had never had a serious boyfriend. She was overweight with enormous breasts, and she desperately wanted to be tall and slim. Sadly, the men she attracted seldom took her seriously. The initial meeting was never a problem, but the commitment was. She liked to spend time with her girlfriends on a Friday night and dance on Thursdays and Saturdays, funds allowing because a Receptionist's wages barely covered her expenses. Jade had been dancing for about a year now and was pretty good, which pleased her, but the thing she enjoyed most was the social life that came with it. The evenings at Club Cubanica were great fun because she had an excellent choice of dance partners. Plus, her collection of men's phone numbers had grown over the last year, and scrolling through her contacts had become a habit. Jade's deep fear of rejection stopped her from contacting them, but she sent the occasional text to say Happy Christmas or Happy Birthday because remembering her friends was crucial.

Jade realised that being everyone's best friend took time and effort, so she had learned to be a great listener. Her friends thought she was fun to be around, but she was unhappy with her weight. Jade had never met a man who respected her and had convinced herself that her body was the issue. Her extra pounds wouldn't shift even with regular dancing, and she was addicted to fizzy drinks which she wanted to give up but found it impossible to change her habits.

Photographs were also a problem because being well-liked, her friends frequently took pictures of her. Jade preferred to take selfies of just her head and shoulders and upload them to Facebook, but she was continually looking for better images. She was excited about going out with the girls tonight, but she was scared to look at her bank balance! Where had her wages gone? Could she cut down on non-essentials? The French weekender wasn't far away, and she still had to make the last payment at the end of the week. Dancing was necessary, so that was impossible to change. It was also difficult to look her best when her wardrobe needed constant updating! She had grown out of most of her dresses and preferred loose trousers with long tops unless the dress was incredibly flattering.

Jade's flat which was close to the town centre, was perfect because she could walk everywhere. There were some great bars five minutes away at the Marina. Jade typically drank a bottle of wine every Friday night, and at the end of the evening, one of the girls would call her a taxi or walk her home. To her relief, her friends always looked after her. She was unsure why she got drunk, it was just one of those things, and besides, everyone needed to chill. It was stressful being a receptionist with the staff and clients on at her all day long. If she repeated the words, 'One moment please, one more time,' on a Friday afternoon, she would explode, so a few glasses of wine set her up for the weekend, and she could switch off until Monday!

Jade shut down her computer. Her desk looked tidy, so she quickly found her jacket. Due to her work's strict mobile policy, her phone had been off all afternoon! Some of her colleagues were still busy working, so she shouted goodbye and headed for the door. Many of them stayed until past 6 pm, which perplexed her. They must earn more money; she thought as she slipped on her coat.

'Ah, you're off now are you, Jade?' asked Brian, the Head Partner of the firm of Solicitors, who had just walked into the Reception Area for water.

'Yeah, I've got to go because I'm meeting friends tonight', she replied.

'No salsa, or is that tomorrow?'

Salsa's always Thursdays. You ought to give it a try, it's fun!' she replied, giving Brian a little smile.

'What me? No, I've got two left feet, but it sounds great. Maybe one day.'

'Come with me then. Just let me know, and we can sort something out,' Jade replied as she opened the door.

She liked Brian. He was always grateful for

her efforts. Her wages were low, but working in town gave her access to the shops during her lunch break. As Jade closed the door, she noticed it was only a few minutes past five, which was fantastic. She quickly turned on her phone and immediately noticed a text appear from Cameron. He had never sent her a message before, and for a moment, her heart stopped. He occasionally chatted to her at salsa, as did everyone, but there had never been any romantic interest. After all, Cameron was gorgeous and could choose the woman he wanted.

Jade quickly read the text and was even more surprised.

'Hi, Jade, can you call me, please? C,' she smiled, then quickly pressed his number. Her heart pounded with anticipation, and she hoped he wasn't playing around.

'Hi, Cameron, it's Jade. You sent a text?'

'Oh hi, I wondered if you wanted to go out for a pizza, or something else to eat then hang out for a bit? I can meet you around 7?' Cameron asked.

Jade's heart continued to beat fast! Perhaps he did like her, but she didn't know how to respond to him. Why would Cameron want to spend time with her? It seemed strange, but she wasn't going to let this opportunity go. Wow, if only the girls knew about this, they would be dead jealous. Her answer had to be yes, even if she was trembling in her shoes. Her feet ached, but if she gave them a long soak as soon as she got home; hopefully, they'd recover! She wanted to look her best for Cameron. Who knows what they would do after the meal, perhaps find somewhere to dance?

Two hours later, after she had soaked her feet, Jade found a fabulous red silk dress, which was flattering and with the addition of some jewellery, she felt reasonably happy with her appearance. It wasn't long before she found herself sitting with Cameron at a Pizza restaurant in the heart of the Marina. Jade had already drunk two glasses of wine, and her meal was half-eaten.

'Are you enjoying that?' he asked.

'Yeah, it's good. I love it here. I come here with my friends, then we go for drinks, sometimes a club, although a lot of them are rough now.'

Cameron didn't know what to say, so he smiled and drank his beer.

Jade wondered why he'd invited her, if he didn't have much to say, and began to feel uncomfortable. She would prefer to leave rather than have him stare at her while she ate, which was embarrassing. He had only ordered a small pizza which had disappeared in no time. It wasn't as if they were in a hurry?

'Do you think I'm fat?' she eventually asked.

'Fat, of course not. I find you quite sexy. I'm not fond of skinny women because they often have hang-ups. Cuddly women are a lot more affectionate.'

'Really', replied Jade, who was now beaming. Cameron quickly poured her another glass of wine and continued to be courteous.

'Whereabouts do you live Jade? You've had rather a lot to drink. Can I walk you home? Maybe watch a movie together on Netflix? I've got it on my phone. It's a little small, but we could sit close.'

'I'm five minutes from here on Ivory Street. I can manage to walk thanks; I always get like this when I'm out with the girls. I never drink when I'm dancing, or I don't dance well.'

'I don't think any of us can! Do you dance Cuban, or crossbody?' asked Cameron, who had suddenly perked up at the mention of dancing.

'Cameron, you dance with me every week. I'm surprised you don't remember how I dance! Cuban, I prefer it. I'm not good at keeping things in straight lines. I like to revolve.'

'Like a revolving door, you mean?'

'Yeah, like a revolving door, but I doubt I'd fit through one of those,' replied Jade, as she began to relax.

'Well, I'd like to walk you home because if you can't dance in a straight line, I doubt you can walk in one?' continued Cameron. He knew he was teasing her, which always brought out the best in women, and Jade appeared to like it because she was becoming more friendly.

'I'm not ready to go yet. I need my dessert. Do you want one, or shall we share?'

'Yeah, we can share if you like. You order it, but we'll need separate spoons.'

When the dessert finally arrived, Cameron let Jade have it all because he didn't have a sweet tooth and he was conscious of his weight. He continued to tease Jade with little jokes, but as her laughing became louder, he didn't know where to look, so he quickly asked for the bill and shuffled her out of the restaurant. His arm was tight around her so he could steer her in the direction he wanted.

'Which way is it Jade? You lead," he said suddenly releasing his arm.

'What I lead! Are you sure about that?'

'Yeah, I am, but don't step on my feet, because I'm wearing Cuban heels,' he replied, jokingly.

As they walked, Cameron slipped his hand in his pocket and pulled his phone which he'd left on silent. He noticed that there were now three missed calls from Linda followed by a text which said, come around about 8, that will give me time to cook dinner. It was now 8.30 pm, and Cameron felt a little annoyed because Jade had begun to bore him. Did anything intelligent come out of her mouth, or did she enjoy putting herself down all evening? He didn't care if she was fat, he wanted to fuck her then get over to Linda's. If only he'd checked his phone earlier, but it was awkward when he was topping up Jade with wine! Why had she ordered that desert, it wasn't as if she needed it and it made them late!

Cameron put his phone back in his back pocket. He realised this could soon get tricky because he'd have to come up with an excuse to leave early. Hopefully, he'd be away by ten, because he didn't want to be any later.

'What's up, is something wrong?' asked Jade, who had noticed Cameron looking at his phone with a worried expression.

'No, everything's fine, just checking the time. Do you have any coffee? This flat is lovely Jade, very cosy.'

'Yes, of course, I have coffee. I love my flat. It's so near town and work.'

'And do you have a comfy bed because I'm exhausted?'

'I don't know about that Cameron. I can make coffee, but I'm not sure about anything else. I'm not used to visitors apart from the girls. You're a lot older than me, and that's frightening. I thought we were going to watch a film?'

'You are frightened, of what?' he asked, as he suddenly slid his arms around her. 'God your thighs are gorgeous', he said, lifting her skirt. 'Let's go and lie down together, and I'll show you what it feels like to have a real man.'

Five minutes later, after Jade had tactfully jumped into her bed, while Cameron was in the bathroom, she could feel him thrusting deep inside her, and she wasn't sure if she liked it. She preferred to look at someone's face than have her head face down in a pillow. He got off her and rolled her over. Let's look at these titties, wow, you're every man's heaven, Jade,' he said, starting again. Jade slid her fingers along Cameron's very smooth, toned body and cried. She desperately wanted love, and this didn't feel like it! Sometime later, Cameron looked up and wiped her tears.

'What's the matter, Jade. Was it the drink?'

'Don't worry. I'm just not used to it.'

'What you're not used to drinking?

'No, I'm not used to sex.'

'Oh, well, you're fantastic. You're probably not getting enough! I'd love to come again if you can put up with me?'

'Really, you don't think I'm fat?'

'You're not fat. You're cuddly, and I like cuddly. I hope you don't mind, but I must leave soon because I promised a mate, I'd help set up some speakers for tomorrow.

'Well, ok, thanks for walking me home!'

'We had fun, didn't we? I'll call you soon. I'll just take a quick shower if that's ok?'

'I'll get you a towel,' replied Jade as she headed to the airing cupboard.

While Cameron was in the bathroom, he hastily took out his phone. It was 9.45 pm, and Linda would have given up on him, which was a shame because he could eat something else now his pizza had worn off, so he quickly messaged to say, sorry, a mate asked him for help with something urgent, and his mobile battery died. Could he still pop over for coffee, or was it too late?

Linda received the text and opened it straight away. She hadn't made anything special to eat because she was annoyed. It was just her usual casserole in the slow cooker, even so, it wouldn't last much longer. Cameron was already messing her around. First, he wanted to see her and then he disappeared when she didn't reply immediately. Well, hard luck, she'd already eaten, and there was only a tiny portion left!

'Ok then, come now, but don't stay too long because I decided to have an early night,' she replied. Cameron felt relieved and placed the towel on Jade's radiator. He thought her flat was homely and he would have stayed longer if he had the time. Jade was far more of a catch than he anticipated. It had never crossed his mind that she was worth seeing until today. He'd seen her cleavage at salsa, who hadn't, and he'd always thought what a great arse, but he'd never taken her seriously. He had often seen her drinking at salsa, and she didn't drink and dance! The girl had a bad memory!

Cameron walked to Jade's front door and quickly put on his shoes. He kissed Jade boldly on the lips and went to retrieve his parked car from outside the pizza restaurant. He then set off to Linda's. What luck, a simple excuse, a little juggling and it was possible to see two sexy women in one night! He still wasn't sure if Jade fitted that description, but there was something about her. She made him feel safe like his mum, which was a little weird. In contrast, Linda was more like a teacher, which he also loved, especially when she dominated him. He loved her being in control.

Linda was bony, angular with short hair, but she was also a sexy squirmy fish. He liked Linda and Jade, and he'd enjoy taking them both, for a while, because he was interested in some of the other dancers. The yoga teacher looked fit, but she hardly talked, which intrigued him. She seemed perfect, too good to be true, but he was sure part of her was reckless. He hoped he'd find out soon before someone else did!

Linda opened the door and smiled. Cameron apologised for being late and Linda thought he appeared genuinely sorry. She then pulled him into the hallway, closed the front door and pinned him against the wall.

'You're such a naughty boy. I'll make you pay for this,' she whispered.

He loved it and ran his hands over her breasts.

'You've forgiven me then?' he asked.

'Not entirely, but I've saved you some dinner. Are you hungry?'

'I'm starving, but let's eat later!' he said, grabbing her buttocks.'

CHAPTER 3
BALANCED AND HAPPY
SARAH

Sarah prepared her yoga class. She planned her lessons to fit with her students' needs, which worked well. They started with a few simple stretches using their arms and legs, then moved on to cat-cow, downward dog and various balances. Sarah had numerous exercises but selected a few new ones each week to challenge her pupils. Her class were a keen group that had grown over the last few months. They were mainly women, with a few eager husbands who had recently joined. Sarah hoped the males would grow in number over time because it was a better balance. The harassed husbands rushed home from work to join the class, and despite seeming a little stressed on arrival, they always commented on how fantastic they felt when they finished. Sarah's lessons were usually an hour three times a week. She also attended a local gym, but this had lapsed in favour of salsa!

Sarah loved dancing. She often wished that she'd trained in dance rather than yoga. Her mother, who was in her late sixties, was also a yoga teacher who still practised at home. Sarah was amazed at how physically fit her mother was, which had encouraged her to follow a similar path teaching yoga and more recently, meditation. Her mum was also a trained reflexologist who still had a few regular clients. Sarah noticed she was continually busy but appeared healthy and happy. Her father, a keen golfer, also kept fit. Somehow the combination of her mother's occasional yoga retreats and her father's trips to Spain for golf holidays worked well for them. He always appeared to have fun even if he spent most of his time hitting the balls into bunkers!

Several years ago, Sarah trained with the British Wheel of Yoga. She made a good living through her classes and had gained an excellent reputation by recommendation. She was known and respected in her local community. Before Sarah danced, she spent her time with a few good friends, but her social circle was small. Now it was gradually expanding, which pleased her. It was a challenge to plan her classes in between her activities, but Sarah had become an expert at juggling the different aspects of her life. Her yoga class had flown by this evening, and she hastily grabbed her coat to return home to her small

Victorian terrace house in Sunnyside Avenue. She wanted to get ready for salsa and didn't want to miss the start of the class. Her home was small with oodles of charm and many original features which Sarah loved. It was ideal for her and Tiger. Her life was good, but she had recognised her need for more fun.

Sarah quickly showered and changed then got ready to dance. Her wardrobe was full of beautiful dresses, but she opted for a pair of short denim shorts with a loose top because it was sweltering. Trousers would stick to her legs in this heat and be very uncomfortable on the dance floor! Sarah's straight blonde hair had looked the same for years, but she was happy with it, so she never considered a change. If she wore it up, it seldom stayed in place. It appeared slightly boyish, but it was best left loose and free. Her slim toned legs looked beautiful in shorts, and jealous onlookers frequently admired them, but she knew the work required to maintain a healthy body! Anyone could have great looking legs if they wanted to put the effort in!

Tiger was rubbing his face against the arm of the sofa, so she sat down to give him a fuss. Her cat loved gentle scratches behind his ears and purred loudly. She felt mean leaving him on his own because he was old now and her best friend! They had lived together for twelve years. She gently removed him from her lap and placed him on the rug beside her.

'I'll be back later,' she said softly as she quickly checked his food and water. Sarah decided not to cycle but to take her car because she was late. Fortunately, the car park was close to the dance club, so it wasn't far to walk.

Sarah went on her own to Club Cubanica. The girls always talked to her when she arrived, but she didn't consider them close friends. A few of the dancers knew that Sarah worked as a yoga teacher, but the salsa crowd preferred to talk about topics that didn't interest her. Since Sarah discovered how to still her mind, she didn't need to be involved because she wanted to live a simple life away from dramas. The French weekender had been a challenging decision, but in the end, she had decided to go. The Yurt would allow her space because the other dancers were camping in tents. Jade and Linda were friendly, so she could cope with their chat for a few days if she stayed grounded and remembered to meditate!

As she arrived outside the front of Club Cubanica, the sound of salsa music quickly filled her ears. They were already playing one of her favourite tracks, La Vida Es Un Carnaval which was extremely lively and it immediately put her in the mood to dance! She was a little late for the warm-up, but people tended to arrive late! They always danced in lines, at the start, which was terrific fun.

Sarah hadn't been dancing long, so she

usually stood behind someone good so she could follow. After the warm-up there would be social dancing, then the teacher would begin the Cuban lesson, where they went through various sequences, followed by a group Rueda. Sarah loved Rueda because it was fast, and they rapidly changed partners. If one person went wrong, it could mess up the whole circle, so they had to keep going. If disaster struck, they would often be in stitches, and there was no choice but to smile! Over the last couple of months, Sarah had learned the best course of action was not to go wrong in the first place, or if by any chance she did, to quickly get back in time ready to grab the next partner before they got away! Last week they learned Coca-Cola, which was fun. She was unlikely to forget the name, although she didn't drink it!

As Sarah entered the bar, she noticed Cameron sitting on a bar stool with Linda and Jade on either side of him. They appeared to be drinking. Sarah didn't want to appear anti-social, but she wasn't interested in being around drinkers. She usually brought along a bottle of water. How could anyone focus on dancing when alcohol changed your vibration, she thought. As Sarah walked past Cameron and the two women towards the dance floor, Cameron lifted his hand to say hello. She quickly waved back and noticed his short black dreadlocks poking out beneath his trilby hat. He looked sexy, confident and intriguing. She breathed and remembered the negative feelings associated with dramas and decided it would be better to keep away. It became apparent to her weeks ago that Cameron was an attractive man, but he seemed extremely popular with the women and how could that be healthy? Some men were women magnets with energy that was impossible to escape! She still held the memory of a painful relationship that had ended five years ago. They had talked about settling down and having a family together, but everything changed. How could she have been so wrong? If only she had listened to her intuition, but in those days, she was so unaware. Now, with the help of yoga and meditation, she had awakened. Sarah found it tempting to be in Cameron's social circle but risking her sense of self when she had worked so hard made her uncomfortable. Sarah still occasionally thought about Julian, when his aftershave lingered in the air from another man! Yet, ninety per cent of the time, she was free of him. Thank goodness she had trained her mind. Drift offs or fantasies were dangerous places to be. If she entered that world, she would soon start to tell herself stories.

Cameron and Linda suddenly appeared on the dance floor, while Jade was obliviously chatting on her mobile, drinking wine. Sarah finished her water and, took up her position in the line. She didn't want to miss the fun when she had already missed the start. Cameron then retreated from Linda and walked towards her, taking up his position directly in front of her.

Sarah surveyed the shape of Cameron's toned body. His tight-fitting black trousers flattered his perfect buttocks. Was that a handkerchief that hung out of his pocket? The trend had swept through many men at salsa, which was good because it meant they could wipe away their sweat instead of dripping over the ladies! At some well-attended dances, the hosts also provided deodorant, which was fantastic. The organisers encouraged the dancers to keep as fresh as possible. Hence, a few of the guys also brought along a second or even third shirt! Sarah took in a deep breath. She was glad the men kept fresh because it encouraged her to dance.

It wasn't long before Sarah found her natural rhythm and style. She was quick and agile, and her arms wanted to move as fast as her legs. As soon as the warm-up was over, Cameron turned and grabbed her hand firmly before she had the chance to move away. He led her into a sequence of simple steps. Sarah was mesmerised but held her composure as she tried to catch his eye through their rapid turns and spins. Was he avoiding her eye contact? Perhaps he was afraid? Surely not, that was madness; she thought feeling a little put-out. The music gradually ended, and she took a few long deep breaths. Yoga helped her dance because she knew how to breathe correctly, and she smiled.

'Thanks,' said Cameron. He then removed his hat, wiped around his face and neck, replaced it and walked away.

'Thanks', thought Sarah was that an attempt to be courteous? She hastily walked over to buy another bottle of water at the bar and noticed Jade wiggling towards him with an outstretched hand. Cameron's body quickly turned away to survey the other women in the room. She felt a little sorry for Jade, who had a distinct look of disappointment on her face. He wasn't interested in dancing with her tonight!

'Bachata, I love it! Do you want to dance Sarah?' asked a voice behind her? Sarah turned abruptly to notice George hovering in her space. She reluctantly took George's hand because he was often overzealous in his dancing. He had hurt her shoulders before by wrenching her arms, but surely, he couldn't go wrong with Bachata?

Two hours later, Sarah angrily hobbled to her car. George was so damn clumsy. He'd trodden on her feet three times. Not only that, but he had sweated profusely and hadn't considered changing his shirt or doing the hanky thing! What would she look like in her yoga class tomorrow with bruises all over her feet? As she got into her car to drive home, her usual cool had turned into anger. Salsa was her passion, and she didn't intend to give it up but couldn't these dancers be more aware? Some of them had no perception of the other dancers' whereabouts. Maybe they should dance at home instead of attending a class where they were clumsy and found it hard to make eye contact! Sarah took some long deep breaths, in through the nose and out through the mouth until she had steadied herself.

When she got in, she would soak her feet and, hopefully, they would recover by tomorrow! Sarah continued to feel angry, which was unusual because it usually quickly went away. She wasn't sure if she was more annoyed at George for her injury or Cameron for making her feel invisible. I may be a yoga teacher, but I still feel passion, Sarah thought angrily. Even if she had an attraction for Cameron, I'm not going there not after last time when my heart was in pieces. Sarah had decided a long time ago, that it was unwise to show interest in men. She had stupidly worn her heart on her sleeve, and it was now in a secret drawer. By now, she hoped to have children. It was painful to reflect. Apart from her yoga classes, she spent most of her time talking to Tiger, who frequently disappeared? Was it time to admit that she was lonely?

There had been a distinct smell about Cameron that took her back. Was that coconut oil or something else? Yes, that was probably it. Sarah could still smell it now, and it intrigued her. She wanted to touch his skin and slide her hands down his arms to feel his strength. If only he would hold and kiss her not just in a casual way but in a way that meant something. It had been so long.

Her clothes lay heaped in a chair. It was far too late to think about taking a shower now. She felt ready for bed. The thing she felt for Cameron was most likely lust, but the man wouldn't even make eye contact! As Sarah pulled back her bedcovers, she immediately noticed Tiger curled up in a ball. He purred as she came close. 'I thought you were out hunting. If only cats could talk!' she said.

CHAPTER 4
THANK GOD IT'S FRIDAY

Jade felt relieved it was Friday. She was looking forward to spending the weekend dancing both salsa and kizomba. It was now her lunch hour, so Jade checked the time on her mobile and hurriedly walked into the central part of the town to search for clothes. As she hastily entered one of her favourite stores, Jade noticed the garments seemed reasonably priced and, she hoped there would be enough time to try things on. Her sandwiches had disappeared at breakneck speed before she left, which always worked well when she went shopping because her lunch hour always flew by!

Jade had just sent a message to Cameron to ask when he was free. She kicked herself for sending it because she wanted to wait until he contacted her, but apart from seeing him last week at Club Cubanica, he hadn't been in touch since they were together. It was now the following Friday lunchtime, and Jade had started to worry. Hopefully, she'd find someone to take her to the kizomba event if there wasn't a train? When it came to dancing in different locations, it was more convenient to ask for lifts because there was little public transport.

It was a warm day, and Jade worked her way along a row of sleeveless tops. She didn't want to wear anything dull, it had to be bold or glitzy and show a little cleavage but not ridiculously low, or it would be unsafe to dance! Jade put a few items back on the rail and sighed. Her problem was she was short in the body with broad shoulders and hips. Didn't they make clothes for girls like her or just skinny bitches! Her phone buzzed, and she jumped because she didn't expect to receive a reply so quickly.

'Hey Jade, it's good to hear from you. Can I meet you tomorrow afternoon? How about coffee at yours? I haven't got long because I need to help set up the Kizomba gig around six, but I can come around 4?'

Jade thought for a few minutes, 4 pm, she'd be at home, but having coffee at her flat would probably lead to sex. She felt a huge attraction to Cameron, and she wanted to see him. She had thought of nothing but them together since he came to the flat. Cameron was in a class of his own, not like the other fumbling idiots. He was intelligent, fit, and a great dancer with an overwhelming presence around him. He also made her feel sexy, but she had hoped that if they met again, he would take her on a date.

Jade put down the sensible tops and decided to go for a more daring option. Her boobs wouldn't fall out so long as she didn't shoulder shake! Besides Cameron would love it if they had, he'd told her they were the most beautiful he'd ever seen! She smiled, then texted him back, 'Yes ok, see you later, but don't be late because I'm going to the Kizomba night too.' If he was going, then she was. She would find a way of getting there, come hell or high water!

'If you buy another top, you get one free,' said the girl at the counter. 'They're two for one.'

'How many have I got?' asked Jade, who had lost herself in a vision of Cameron.

'You've got five, put them here if you like and get one more.'

Jade grabbed another top, then noticed some sparkly silver trousers that were a little long in the leg.

'I'll have these trousers as well. Do you have them in a short leg?' Jade asked, then smiled at the girl.'

'No, we only do long legs in those. Do you still want them?'

'Long leg, yeah, I'll take them and cut a bit off!' answered Jade as she glanced at her watch.

'That will be £65.99,' said the girl.

Jade took out her credit card and handed it to the shop assistant. Her receptionist's salary couldn't keep pace with her spending habits, and she still had to buy wine and snacks for Cameron's visit tomorrow. Perhaps she could start to charge for painting nails, she thought, as the knot in her stomach grew.

Fortunately, there were no missed calls on her return to the office, and no one had noticed she was ten minutes late. First thing tomorrow she would do her nails so they would look great for Cameron's visit. She'd wear the trousers tomorrow night. She thought they'd be great for France, but they were ideal for Kizomba. Jade desperately wanted to look good for Cameron and appear stunning in the evening! She couldn't wait to see him again. It was hard to believe that such a good-looking man was interested in her. She wondered how long it would be before she could tell her Facebook friends that she was 'In a relationship,' wow, what would they think? Most of them would be envious because Cameron was drop-dead gorgeous!

A call came in on line one and Jade returned to reality. She immediately clicked on the screen to see if Mr Wilson was in his office, but she hadn't seen him return from lunch.

'I'm sorry, Mr Wilson isn't in his office, right now. He's probably still at lunch. Can I take a message, or ask him to call you back?'

'It's Francesca, his wife. I thought you knew my voice Jade,' she replied abruptly.

'Oh, sorry, Mrs Wilson, you sounded a little different today?'

'Please can you ask Brian to call me when he returns? It's urgent.'

'Yeah sure,' she said, as she suddenly realised her manner had grown a little casual! Where was Brian? He was usually back by now, she thought, as her energy started to plummet to the ground! I'm not sure where he now, but I'll tell him you called,' she repeated like a parrot.

At two-thirty, Brian walked through the large glass door and helped himself to some water from the drink dispenser. Jade thought he appeared slightly rude because he had his back to her, so she leaned forward and said, 'Brian, your wife called about fifteen minutes ago. She told me it was urgent.'

Brian immediately swung around to face her, and as he did, Jade could smell a distinctive perfume around him that she hadn't encountered in the office before. Jade knew her perfumes. Her friends often said that she would be happier selling them than answering calls all day which Jade was inclined to agree with, mostly when the clients were impatient or rude! 'Ah yes, Tiffany,' Jade muttered, at least it smelt like it. Jade loved that smell. She'd know it anywhere.

Brian turned around to look her in the eye. 'Sorry, I'm a little late, but I met a client for lunch, and it went on longer than I intended. I'll ring her straight back, but it probably isn't urgent, just a drama over one of the kids!'

Jade smiled to herself, whoever Brian had

met for lunch, she had great taste in perfume! It would be intriguing to find out! Work had suddenly become a lot more interesting. Was it just business, or was Brian taking someone out for lunch? She had been into his office a few times recently, and on seeing her, he had quickly changed the subject or ended the conversation. The light which indicated that he was on the phone would often stay on for over an hour, which meant that he was making some very long calls. Jade sighed. She needed to focus until the end of the day because there she had a good weekend ahead. Seeing Cameron was exciting, but Jade also wanted to practise her French. She knew the basics and could now ask for a glass of wine which was a great start!

'Un verre de vin s'il vous plait? Or, something like that,' she whispered. Her pronunciation was a bit iffy, but she'd get there. Maybe Linda could help. She knew French, but she appeared stressed lately. Or there was Sarah; who was the quiet, all-knowing, type. Sarah was always calm, although she didn't talk to the group much. Everyone was amazed that she was going on the trip. It wasn't as if it was a yoga retreat; there would be a lot of drinking, but she seemed keen to camp, and that was the part she dreaded!

After a barrage of calls, Jade got away from the office at five and locked the door behind her. One of the partners had left early, but they usually arrived at some ridiculously early time in the morning. Brian was still there and had asked her to lock the Reception door as she left, so the public didn't wander in.

Jade had her handbag over her shoulder. She was also carrying the bag of clothes that she'd acquired at lunchtime as she quickly headed off in the direction of her flat. Her phone started to ring. It was Linda, 'Hey Jade, are you are going to the Kizomba event tomorrow? I was thinking of going, but I don't want to go on my own. Jade was silent She had wanted to go on her own so Cameron would feel sorry for her and ask her for more dances, but how could she when it was impossible to get there by public transport!

'I'm going, but I'm not sure what time I'll get there,' replied Jade.

'Shall I pick you up then, or meet you there?' replied, Linda kindly.

'No, I'll meet you there. I'm swamped tomorrow so I might be late?'

'Busy, come on Jade, who is he? I've seen you texting. You are hiding something. You can tell me?'

'No, I can't because he would kill me and I don't want to, not yet anyway, but all I can say is he's gorgeous and fantastic in bed.'

'Now you're making me jealous', Linda replied laughing.

'I thought you had a lovely husband who is great with your kids and took you on exotic holidays?' said Jade, sounding surprised.

'Well, he is all of that. It's complicated. You wouldn't understand.'

'Yeah, I saw that on your Facebook status! I thought you must have another man or something?'

'Don't be daft. When would I have time for that, besides one man is enough even if he no longer rocks my boat?'

'Rocks your boat?'

'Yeah, see, I said, you wouldn't get it!'

'Ah, I get it; he doesn't do it for you?'

'Something like that! Do you want me to pick you up or not? It sounds like an excuse to me?' asked Linda.

Jade stopped to push the button on the Zebra crossing then quickly walked across the road. She knew she was a chatterbox, but she always paid attention to cars.

'Ok, yeah, come and pick me up at eight please so we can get there around nine. Nothing will happen until then.'

'I can't do Kizomba,' said Linda.

'Oh well, you've just got to relax and let the man guide you and you'll be fine. There is a male saidi and a female saidi, but I get them confused. Some of the guys tell me to lean into them and close my eyes.'

'Close my eyes? Well, I'll watch for a few dances, then give it a go. Salsa is more of my thing. To be honest, I'm not sure about all this fumbling in the dark thing!'

'Oh, I'm great at that,' replied Jade and began to laugh.

Linda laughed back 'See you tomorrow. I'll be outside at 8 pm, and I'll hoot my horn. It's hard to park outside yours, so be quick!' She was concerned that Jade would keep digging into her personal life and within no time at all, everyone would know about her affair, including her husband! Why would she risk everything for a man who didn't bother to turn up when he promised? She must either be mad or menopausal! If Cameron were an animal, he would be a panther because you could never hear him coming, but he could certainly run away fast! It didn't bear thinking about because if he left, she knew that part of her life would be over, the part which brought excitement! She was primarily a woman, not just a housewife and mother. A passionate woman who had needs, but why was it so complicated?

The shower had been running for several minutes, so Linda jumped in. Her new clothes were already hanging in her wardrobe. She thought it would be fun to wear one of the French dresses, tomorrow night because it would look modern, fresh and appealing. There was always competition for Cameron's attention, and she'd noticed Sarah had been watching him lately, which made her uncomfortable.

Fuck him. He's stealing my life. I hate him!

No, I don't hate him, I despise him. There were no words to describe how she felt. She walked into the kitchen to make coffee and let Peanut outside. If this wasn't selling her soul, what was? Linda turned on the oven and put in the casserole that she prepared earlier. Chicken. sweet potatoes, green beans and lentils, Adrian loved it. He would be home from work around 6 pm and would likely drone on about his annoying work colleagues throughout dinner. Then he'd fall asleep watching the news, and she'd disappear to bed.

Linda let Peanut back in and wiped his paws. Thank God, she had the dog. He always greeted her enthusiastically, and coming back home to his wagging tail was a joy. She dreaded telling Adrian about the kizomba night because they hadn't spent any time together for weeks. She didn't want to miss out though, so he'd have to lump it.

CHAPTER 5

NOT THIS AGAIN

LINDA

Linda turned over. She had forgotten that Adrian lay next to her because he was seldom home, but today his early morning snoring had been unusually loud. He had also shuffled towards her and had laid on her side the bed. Linda decided her best course of action was to lie motionless and continue sleeping, but she realised Adrian had other plans when his hand started to stroke the top of her thigh. Her heart raced, and she began to feel a sense of panic. The word menopause usually worked fine. What was he doing? Linda felt tired and was certainly not ready to get up, but she slowly manoeuvred to the edge of the bed and stood up.

'I'm going to get some tea,' she announced. She didn't want to see the look of disappointment on Adrian's face, so she avoided eye contact. It wouldn't change a thing. It was nearly eight o clock, and Peanut would need to go out for a pee. He was an old dog now, so she had to make a move eventually!

'Can you fetch the paper,' replied Adrian in a muffled voice. He sounded annoyed, but Linda knew he'd perk up after breakfast because he always did. If she didn't appear with the tea and newspaper, he'd take a shower then come down. That was their routine, and it had always worked. After breakfast, Adrian would clear away the dishes while she took Peanut for a walk. He would occasionally come with them, but catching up with the paper was his priority. Adrian was predictable, but manageable if left to his own devices.

Linda picked the paper up from the mat, which surprisingly was still in one piece. It was often soggy if Peanut got to it first! Their dog usually entertained himself, but today it was apparent that he'd not moved from his basket. Poor, old boy, Linda said as she went over to stroke their faithful old dog. Peanut was a beautiful golden retriever with gorgeous locks. He wagged his tail as she approached and directed him through the conservatory door to the garden. It appeared to be another beautiful day, which would be great for a short walk down by the brook, she thought smiling. The kettle had boiled, and Linda placed some bread in the toaster. She then laid out some cereals, a toast rack, marmalade and coffee cups on the dining room table. The early morning sun was streaming through the open windows, which made the space look cosy, warm, and inviting.

Adrian always read the Telegraph. He liked to keep up with the political news. He said he wanted to run as a local councillor, but he often said these things and seldom followed through! Linda heard the water stop running and realised that Adrian was out of the shower. At least he wasn't waiting for her to return to bed! He slowly walked down the stairs then sat down for breakfast, then unfolded the paper to glance at the headlines before pouring them both a coffee.

'Oh, the paper's intact', he said smiling.

'Yes, poor Peanut, he wasn't interested in moving out of his basket, today,' she replied with a smile.

'Do you think there's something the matter with him? Are you still taking him out?' Adrian asked.

'Yes of course, but he's old. I'll take him shortly. I always take him down by the brook on Saturdays, don't, I?'

'I don't know Linda. I'm so seldom here. I don't know what you do. It would be nice if we could spend some time together while I'm home. Did you say something about dancing tonight?'

'Yes, I'm going out with Jade. You know, I've mentioned her before, the girl who works as a

Receptionist for Tomlinson and Wilson.

'Ah, yes, I know Brian, he comes to our network meetings.

'You said she was bored with her job and wanted more money or something?'

'Did I, yes maybe. Jade loves clothes and often says she would be better off working in a boutique or selling perfume, which appears to be her second love.'

'Second love, you, women! Well, they are a brilliant firm, so I doubt that she would be treated that well, elsewhere,' continued Adrian as he topped up their coffee.

'Thanks', she said and smiled again

'I wouldn't go tonight, but Jade doesn't want to go on her own. She doesn't drive, so if I don't go, she won't be able to get there. I offered to take her because I thought you were away this weekend. I must have the dates of the conference, confused.'

'That's not like you, Linda. I guess it's this menopause thing. They say it's not only flushes, you can also have memory loss.'

'Really, I'm not senile yet!' she joked.

'I know that, far from it! You looked so beautiful this morning. I found it hard to keep my hands off you.'

'I'm sorry,' she said apologetically, as thoughts of Cameron rushed through her mind because he had said something similar!'

'It's ok, you go and enjoy yourself with Jade.

You deserve it, but don't forget we have to be up early to prepare the barbeque tomorrow. What time is Ian coming?'

'Around eleven, I think', she replied.

Linda hadn't forgotten the barbeque. The food was ready in the fridge. It looked as if it was going to be lovely weather all weekend so they would have a good time even if she had to put on her usual happy show. It would be great to see Ian this weekend. It had been months.

Peanut sat by the front door waiting for his walk, so Linda picked up his lead, grabbed a light jacket and was ready to head off, thinking she could always carry her coat if it became hot.

'Come on old boy', she said, as she began to stroke Peanut's head.

They slowly headed along the Avenue to the main road, across a zebra crossing and then took a long lane that led out to the countryside. Brookfield was a beautiful area surrounded by trees, fields, and meadows, which were frequently full of dogs! Linda knew she was lucky living in such a beautiful location, in a comfortable detached house where there was little crime. Her children had benefited from going to good schools.

Fiona left University a couple of years ago after finishing her teaching degree. She was now teaching in Japan. She'd met her partner at the same University, and they had been together for a few years. They both worked in Japan and had managed to get some temporary accommodation. Fiona hoped to be home for Christmas. Linda missed her, but they frequently talked on skype. She knew Fiona was happy, that was the main thing, but Linda didn't want her to remain there because it was so far away. If Fiona went back after Christmas, she would visit. Adrian had already said he couldn't take time off work so she would have to go on her own! Linda found the thought of visiting Japan challenging but exciting as she loved travelling.

Ian lived in London, which was only a short train journey from Suffolk, so they saw him quite regularly. Linda was pleased he was coming home tomorrow even if it was just for the day because he was usually up to his eyes with work. Ian often arrived on a Friday evening and stayed the whole weekend, but it had become impossible due to his workload. He liked to invite some of his old school friends to their family barbeques so they could catch up while he was home. Linda knew there could be an additional four tomorrow, so she had filled the fridge with plenty of food and beer!

The sun was full out, and Peanut was contentedly paddling in the brook, so Linda decided to send Cameron a quick text. The dog wouldn't stray far because sadly, he had more of a plod at eleven years old!

Linda hadn't heard from Cameron since last week. She hoped to have a couple of dances with him later, but he was a popular guy, so there were no guarantees. Kizomba sounded fun. It would make a change from salsa, but salsa was the dance that started her dancing journey, and it was her first love! She wasn't sure if she wanted to be that close to sweaty strangers who may not have a hanky or spare shirt! Was she prudish? She had noticed that some dancers were gentlemen and others appeared to have other notions! She had allowed Cameron into her space, but that was unintentional and not something she planned to repeat!

'Hi Cameron, I'll see you tonight at Kizomba. I'm taking Jade. I hope this is going to be fun. Linda xxx

It was now 23 degrees, and Linda was hot, so she slung her jacket over her arm. Peanut was still enjoying the brook which appeared to be cooling him down. She loved coming here because it was peaceful and allowed her to think. It was now only a week until they went to France. They were flying from Stanstead, and she had already printed her ticket. She thought it would be a good idea to discuss the arrangements with Jade because they were travelling together. They were also picking up Sarah and possibly Cameron on the route, but he had indicated he might go by train as he lived near the station.

Linda didn't particularly want Sarah to come with them because she didn't know her well, but Jade thought Sarah should be part of their group and it would be mean to leave her out! They were taking tents with them, so it was easier to travel to the airport by car and split the costs. Linda knew this trip was going to be different because whenever she went away with Adrian, they stayed in a hotel, and this time she was camping! Fortunately, Sarah had declared herself an expert at tents, having camped at yoga retreats and had offered to help them set up. It would be fun; besides, she could take her home comforts with her. Linda had already paid for a large suitcase and could purchase a blow-up bed in France because it was better to avoid getting a stiff back with four full days dancing! She would also need several pairs of shoes. There was a swimming pool on the site, which sounded fabulous! At last, she could have some fun with Cameron without the constant worrying of Adrian.

Peanut appeared to have had enough paddling and stood still in the brook with a look that said take me home. Linda put him back on the lead, and they started to stroll back slowly, walking in the shade where they could. Peanut looked happy, even if he was a little doddery. He would sleep well this afternoon she thought smiling. Her phone buzzed, and to her surprise, Cameron had already sent a reply to her text.

'Great, see you later.'

Linda stared at his text. It was merely an acknowledgement, not even a kiss. Still, he had said he was busy. Linda realised that she always wanted more from him, but none ever came. He was always busy, travelling for work, dancing or helping various DJs with their equipment or covering as DJ at the occasional gig. Cameron preferred kizomba to salsa. She wondered if it was an addiction because he would sometimes travel miles to different venues. Linda felt slightly annoyed by his dismissiveness and put her phone away.

What was she going to wear? She had now packed her best clothes for the trip and Adrian wouldn't be impressed if she wore something new. He would accuse her of going over the top! What a pain Adrian had been about her going out this evening until he'd discovered his favourite wildlife series on iPlayer. It would keep him busy all evening being an Attenborough fan. When she returned around midnight, he would no doubt be snoring!

CHAPTER 6
DO YOU LIKE KIZOMBA?
LINDA & JADE

Linda bumped the car up onto the kerb outside Jade's flat and left the engine running. She hoped Jade was ready because she had parked on a double yellow line! Her fingers strummed the driver's wheel impatiently as she waited for Jade to appear. Linda looked around. Jade lived in an unfortunate part of the town, but it was convenient. She sometimes wished their house was a little nearer the town centre because it would give her access to more places to eat and dance. When they bought their house twenty-five years ago, they were more concerned with the quality of the schools than their social life. But it was beautiful in Brookfield, and the countryside surrounded it. It was great for Peanut, as there were many lovely walks. In recent weeks the dog walking had been handed entirely to her, not that she minded because she loved their old retriever. He helped her keep fit. However, Linda had noticed that he'd been struggling lately, poor old boy! They'd had him for such a long time that she couldn't imagine life without him.

At last, Jade appeared and hurried towards the car, having realised it was difficult for Linda to stop. Linda noticed that Jade looked stunning in her silver sparkly trousers which caught the evening sun and a red halter neck top which extenuated the top half of her body. She wore a short strappy summer dress, with bold red flowers. It was an old favourite which came out every summer. Her red strappy dance shoes sat on the top of her handbag which complimented her dress.

They quickly set off to the venue, which was about twelve miles away. It was larger than their usual club, having two rooms. The main one was for Kizomba, and the other room was for salsa and bachata. But this evening, they were focusing on learning Kizomba. Linda knew they would most likely throw in a couple of popular Bachata songs in this room too! Linda loved Bachata, it was fun and romantic, yet it allowed a respectful space between partners, at least the old style did because a lot of the new Bachata dancing that she'd come across, had close contact. She loved the bachata version of 'My All.' The lyrics reminded her of her relationship with Cameron and how she had given him everything, which made her emotional. They had danced to the song on so many occasions, and Cameron had always held her close. Linda wondered if people guessed they were lovers? On the other hand, he danced intimately with so many women.

'Are you alright, Linda, you seem a little quiet. You're not your usual bubbly self?' asked Jade as they headed along the A14 to the event.

'Yeah, I'm ok, thanks. I was just thinking about Adrian. He wasn't happy about me coming out tonight, so I felt a little guilty. He's been away all week, and I left him watching television on his own. I did make his favourite meal though, shepherd's pie, which I only make on rare occasions and not in the hot weather! I had a salad, or I would be too heavy to dance!' she replied.

Jade just smiled. Linda's life was so different from hers. She always planned and was so well organised, and they lived in a beautiful area. Linda also had a dog which was something she had always wanted.

'Are you looking forward to France?' asked Jade as she tried to perk her up.

'Yes, of course, I am. It will be fantastic! I bought a new tent last week, one of those pop-up ones, the sort they use at festivals. It will be easier. I've looked at the forecast for our weekender, and there's going to be plenty of sunshine so we will be fine'.

'Yay, sun and fun,' replied Jade.

'Yes, plenty of fun. I hope that my feet can take the punishment. You're a lot younger than me,' replied Linda.

'Ah age is just a number,' said Jade. She wished Linda would cheer up because she wasn't her usual self.

They arrived at the venue, a large sports hall on the edge of the town. Linda was surprised to see so many cars, but she had heard it was a popular place to dance.

It was now 8.45 pm, and the music had already started. Linda locked the car, and they walked into a massive room that had a long bar along one wall. There was also plenty of seating with many tables. They recognised some familiar faces from Club Cubanica and said hello. Linda couldn't see Cameron anywhere, which she found disappointing. Perhaps he had decided not to come? After all her efforts, when Kizomba wasn't her thing?

Jade offered to buy them a drink. Linda accepted and ordered a glass of soda water and lime because her head had to be clear for the drive home. Jade had the same then declared she never drank while dancing. Linda had seen Jade drink many times and just smiled. She didn't want to get into a debate because Jade didn't remember what happened last week! They soon found a table in the corner of the room close to the DJ, which was a little loud for talking and took their coats off. The dance floor was relatively empty, and Linda suddenly noticed Cameron's hat on top of a speaker at the far end of the room. He was dancing with Sarah, and they appeared very involved. Linda noticed their bodies moving together in perfect time with the music. Their soft steps hardly touched the dance floor. Linda looked on with envy at their graceful display and wished it was her. Sarah could Kizomba!

'So that's Kizomba,' she shouted so Jade would hear her, over the music.

'I love this. I want to dance,' Jade replied as she noticed Sarah's glitzy shorts. She looked stunning, and Jade wished that she had worn shorts instead of her sparkly trousers which had been a pain to turn up!

'Why do you like it?' asked Linda, who also wished that she had worn shorts!

'It reminds me of Cameron. I love the way he dances. He has got great rhythm,' answered Jade.

'Yes, he has,' replied Linda, who had decided the best plan was to get up and ask someone else to dance if she was going to survive the evening!

'Is it ok for women to ask men to dance Kizomba?' she asked Jade as she stood up from her chair.

'They kind of expect it,' answered Jade because there aren't enough good male dancers to go around.

Jade vanished for a while, so Linda asked

Mark to dance. His breath usually wreaked of tobacco, and today was no exception. She realised she had made the wrong choice when Mark moved closer and held her tightly. He was wearing a hat today which gave him a bit of an edge, but Linda still thought he was creepy!

'How are you?' Mark muttered over the loud music.

'Yeah, I'm ok, kind of busy.'

'Are you looking forward to France?'

'I'm looking forward to a holiday and dancing with different people. It should be fun,' Linda replied as she created a little distance between them. She was aware their conversation had turned to banter and fell silent. Mark started to vary the routine, and Linda didn't know the steps. She then remembered that if she relaxed and closed her eyes, it was easier to follow, but Linda didn't want to close her eyes while she danced with Mark because he was unpredictable.

'Ok, well, I don't think I'm getting it,' she said to him.

'You are kind of tense. You need to relax and trust the man,' replied Mark as he breathed into her ear.

'I'm kind of done, so see you later.' She knew it was rude, but she could see Cameron was free and she didn't want to miss out.

Cameron had been confidently chatting with his friends, and his elbow was on the edge of the bar as Linda approached him. He then stopped talking, put down his beer and turned towards her.

'Do you know the steps?' he asked.

'No, but I can follow.'

'Close your eyes, lean in and follow my lead, and you won't go far wrong,' he replied.

As Linda moved closer to him, she suddenly realised they were dancing cheek to cheek. The sweat from his face was touching hers, and she could smell the coconut oil on his skin. As he slightly pulled away, she felt his breath on her neck, and they began to merge with perfect timing.

The music finally stopped, and Cameron pulled away.

'Yeah, you did it. You can Kizomba. It's about keeping the rhythm.'

Linda quickly noticed that Jade, Sarah and several others were all waiting to dance with him. She decided to get out of the way so she could observe the goings-on from a comfortable distance. Was it her imagination or was Cameron less interested in her tonight? Whenever she looked over at him, Sarah was in his space. She had enjoyed their dance, but she had to walk over and ask him. Why hadn't he come to find her? If sharing Cameron made her unhappy, was it worth her coming because it had been a drive and for what? Perhaps it was better to stick with salsa because it was less intimate. There was some skill in this dance, but salsa filled her with joy, and Kizomba felt like an excuse to invade her personal space!

Jade returned, and they started discussing the arrangements for France. She noticed that the people who sat at the table behind were unfamiliar. One of the women wore a short red silk dress and was laughing. As she stood up and headed to the bar with her wine glass, she left behind a trail of perfume which Jade instantly recognised as Tiffany! It was weird because it was the smell that surrounded Brian when he returned from lunch a few days ago. Jade's logical side told her that many women wore that perfume, so it had to be a coincidence, but it was odd to notice it twice in one week!

The tall, slim, dark-haired woman returned to her seat with another glass of wine and began to talk loudly. Jade thought she was a woman she had seen on her way to the office, but her hair was different. She was wearing a dress that was so short dancing would be impossible, but the woman appeared more interested in drinking.

'When are you going to bring this man, you've met?' asked the small blonde lady sitting next to her.

Jade's head turned with interest. She knew eavesdropping was rude, but curiosity had got the better of her.

'You mean Brian? No, he's not interested in socials. I've asked him, but he's busy playing happy families, right now. Ours is more of a horizontal relationship if you know what I mean!'

'So, he doesn't do vertical?' asked the blonde, giggling.

Jade realised she was staring at them, so, she quickly turned away, not wishing to appear rude. The music had changed to bachata, which was loud, and their voices became muffled.

'Come on, Jade, get up, please because this is one of my favourite tracks. Let's find someone to dance with,' said Linda, excitedly.

Jade slowly wobbled to her feet. Her silver three-inch dance heels had caused her feet to swell uncomfortably, and she regretted not wearing her lower black leather ones. Why did she slip so much rum into her last three glasses of coke, she wondered, as she made a wobbly beeline towards Cameron for a second dance? Her favourite track was playing. She loved Mariah Carey; her music was ageless.

Since Cameron's initial interest in her, Jade felt more confident, and she had also lost a few pounds which had lifted her spirits. He had texted to ask if he could visit tomorrow afternoon, but she was meeting her friends. Maybe she could meet them in the evening but her saying no to Cameron might be a good idea because she didn't want him to use her. Cameron had whispered something about her thighs earlier. He had also stuck his tongue in her ear as she moved in close. Jade was relieved that no one had noticed because it was a little embarrassing, but she hadn't told him to stop it.

Linda had become tired of dancing. She decided she would be happier at home and had already put on her jacket. It made her miserable watching Cameron dancing intimately with so many attractive ladies, and she needed to get away before her feelings began to show. The music ended, and Jade suddenly appeared.

'Hey, Linda, what's up? You're not leaving, already are you? Aren't you having fun?

'I'm sorry, Jade, but I don't think Kizomba's my bag. I love Bachata, but they aren't playing enough of it. Salsa's my favourite. It always will be. Maybe I'll stick with that.

'Have you had a dance with Cameron? He's a great dancer. Perhaps he's free now?

'Yes, we danced. It's not about the dances Jade, I can't be late because Adrian was annoyed about me coming plus, we have a family BBQ tomorrow, so I've got to be up early.'

'Yeah,' answered Jade, who didn't want to leave. 'Maybe I can get a lift home with someone else. Then you can go. We can talk about France on the phone.'

'Ok I'll stay for the next dance but can you please ask a few people about a lift now, so I can get off because I don't feel great.'

Linda ordered a coffee at the bar and sat down to look at her phone messages. There were two texts from Adrian, one about getting food out of the freezer for tomorrow and a second one that said, please don't be too late tonight, we need to talk. She looked up and noticed Jade talking to Cameron at the bar. She doubted he would take her home because he lived in the opposite direction.

The music ended, and Linda was relieved to be going home. She couldn't explain it, even though the dance event was in a vast hall she felt suffocated by the atmosphere which felt dark and oppressive. She much preferred their usual salsa club, which had a comfortable and relaxed atmosphere.

Jade hobbled over in her silver shoes, which appeared to be causing her pain.

'Hey Linda, you can go if you like because I've got a lift from Cameron,'

Linda's heart sank. It was on the tip of her tongue to say 'Cameron, he lives in a different direction, but realised that the least personal information she discussed with Jade, the better.

'Yeah, he has to come past mine to return the speakers.'

'Ok, well, I'm off now then,' she said, giving Jade a quick kiss on the cheek. As she walked out of the room, she thought about saying goodbye to Cameron, but she couldn't do it. Something didn't feel right. Her heart pounded, and she realised it was a palpitation. Was she blind, had he seen Jade all along? Surely not, but something was wrong. Everywhere she looked, there was a woman pressed up against him, laughing and smiling. Had Cameron been honest about anything? How many women had he pursued when he wasn't with her? She suddenly felt sick, then leaned over to vomit on the concrete next to her car. She had to hold herself together to drive home, but she felt all over the place!

Linda opened her car door. She wanted to sit in her car for a few minutes to contain herself before driving home. There was a bottle of water on the front seat, and Linda took some long slow sips. The drink made her feel a little better, and she felt alright to drive.

It was now 11 o clock, and if she put her foot down, hopefully, she would be home by eleven-thirty. Adrian would still be up then so they could chat. She didn't feel in the mood to talk, let alone discuss anything heavy, but she owed it to him to listen.

Linda walked into the lounge half an hour later to find Adrian fully outstretched on the sofa. The television series he loved was still on the television, and he appeared to have nodded off. Peanut was asleep, stretched out on the floor next to Adrian's feet. He looked very content. The clock ticked on their marble mantlepiece and everything was peaceful.

Linda was very fond of Adrian. She was no longer in love with him, but there was still something between them. Cameron was single, and from what she gathered, he didn't know much about responsibility. He had parents and a brother and sister, but he didn't know what it was like to bring up children. Unlike herself, she was now in her fifties with grown-up children. Would it be better to end her affair now, before things got out of control? For the first time, Linda began to feel ashamed about her feelings for Cameron.

'Hi darling, did you have a good time,' Adrian mumbled sleepily.

'Yes, it was good, but I decided Kizomba wasn't my thing, so I left the event early so we could talk. What do you want to talk about?' she asked in the sweetest tone she could muster. Linda suddenly felt worried about her affair with Cameron. Perhaps one of the neighbours had said something? It was unlikely because he usually asked a friend to give him a lift to the house, or he parked a little distance away. It wasn't as if he came at the same time every week either. Their meetings were irregular.

'Oh, I was thinking, it's been a long time since we took a holiday together and this long weekend in France sounds great. I know I can't dance, but if I come with you, we could maybe book a hotel in the area. Do you want to do this camping thing? It isn't you, is it? It's a bit rough and ready. When was the last time you did that?'

Linda had started to lose herself a little in rough and ready and was trying to pull her thoughts back, but Adrian's words had shocked her. After what felt like ages, she reluctantly replied.

'Adrian, I'm fine about camping. I told you last week that I'd bought a pop-up tent and I'm looking forward to this trip.'

'So, you are going with Jade and who else?'

'I told you a group from our salsa class. I can't change things now because I would let others down; it's all organised. I am picking up Jade and Sarah. I don't mean to be difficult, but I was looking forward to having a long weekend with the girls. Can't we go away another time? If you come, we'll have to find someone to look after Peanut, and that would be difficult. The trip's next weekend.'

Adrian looked disappointed. Linda was surprised that he hadn't said anything until now, but she had a hunch, something was coming. She didn't want him to feel left out, but she needed space to herself. It would be a nightmare if he came. She had to be a little more convincing.

'I don't think you would enjoy it much. You don't know the other people, and you would feel like a fish out of water. Plus, it's going to be hot, and you hate the heat.'

'Yes, I know, but we don't spend much time together, and it would be a chance to meet your friends. I'm sure that I could pick up some basic steps? It would be fun.'

Linda's heart began to race. No, it wouldn't be fun, not for her. She needed to think of a reason for Adrian to stay at home without making him feel unwanted.

'The thing is, Jade just broke up with her boyfriend, and she's distraught, so I promised to keep her company, she needs support. I would let her down if I spend all my time with you.'

'Jade's boyfriend, you've never mentioned that. Do you know him? You said she was, loud, overweight and men took advantage of her.'

'She's been dating Cameron.'

'Cameron, ah yes, you've mentioned him a couple of times. He's that black guy in his forties, isn't he? You see, I do know some of your friends because you've mentioned them. Last night you were muttering Cameron in your sleep. I wondered what you were saying, so I got up close. It must have been something about Jade. Is he going on the trip, that would be difficult for her?'

'Yeah, he's going on the trip, but nobody likes him. He's a womaniser,' Linda replied with her heart racing. Talking about Cameron hadn't been part of her plan when the conversation began, but she had to use him to break free from Adrian. She knew she was sailing close to the wind, and it was becoming very uncomfortable.

'Well, I'd better not come because if he makes a beeline for you, I might end up punching him.'

She was playing with fire, but it was working well, and she hoped that Adrian would soon drop his defences and see sense!

'It's a shame, but I think you're right. You need to look after Jade besides if there a lot of male egos there, I think I'd be better at home with Peanut. I can arrange for a few of my old mates to come over; you know the cricket gang. I feel as if I've given up so much since I started going to all these conferences. My head is always stuck in front of my laptop.'

'Ok, darling, as long as you're sure. We can take a break soon. Go somewhere else, perhaps at the end of October. How about Greece? You know how you like the Greek Islands.'

'That sounds good,' he replied, 'I will look at some places while you are away, then we can book when you're back.

Thank goodness for that, Linda muttered as she went to put the kettle on. She often had herbal tea before she went to bed, but when Linda returned to the lounge, the sofa was empty. Adrian had gone to bed. She decided to sit down and watch a bit of Netflix for an hour. If Adrian had insisted on coming to France, it would have ruined everything. She wouldn't have any time alone with Cameron, and he would have curtailed her dances. It wouldn't have been worth going. She was pleased that he'd swallowed the excuse about Jade. Her friend looked different; lately, she appeared more confident, and her clothes had changed. Was she slimmer? Linda turned her phone back on and immediately saw a text from Cameron.

'I'm not sure why you left Jade on her own, but don't worry, I looked after her!'

Linda's heart sank, and she felt in a very dark place.

What the fuck was he doing? Perhaps she wasn't the only one who played with fire! Had she learned this from him, or had he learned it from her? Linda turned the light off and climbed the stairs. She couldn't bear the thought of sleeping next to Adrian because her head was far too busy. She needed to be alone.

Linda stuck her head into Ian's old bedroom. She had changed the sheets ready for his visit tomorrow. Ian's empty bed appeared so warm and comforting that she climbed in it. After a few minutes, Linda drifted into a peaceful sleep. She awoke in the early hours of the morning, crying and realised that making a decision was easy. They had been together for the last time!

CHAPTER 7
ONE TEXT TOO MANY
BRIAN

Brian glanced at this mobile. He felt hounded by Michele, and he wished that he'd never met her. His friend Adrian had introduced her to him at their May network meeting because she'd been his accountant for years and as her office was practically next door, they decided to meet for lunch. Brian didn't imagine their lunches would soon turn into regular events, including meeting for drinks after work. He fancied Michele, but it wasn't long before he discovered that this lady worked and played hard, and he couldn't keep up with her! Michele frequently called him on his mobile, in the evenings, and when there was no response, she would leave a slurred voicemail. Next, he would get 'I'm sorry, can we talk about it over lunch tomorrow?' Lunch would once again turn into late lunch, or worse than that, an afternoon in bed! Brian was tired of saying, I'm sorry Jade but I'm still stuck in a meeting, and I won't be returning to the office until tomorrow! She wasn't stupid. It wasn't pleasant. If he didn't respond to Michele's messages, she would call again, or worse, turn up at the office and demand to speak to him. He had continually requested that she didn't just turn up because he had regular appointments with clients, plus he didn't want his staff to think something was going on! Michele appeared to have little self-control, and it was too much for him. Surely ten missed calls would test anyone when they were working!

Brian had been married for years. He couldn't remember what dating was like, but he knew this wasn't right. Was his wedding anniversary coming up? He wasn't sure. He would usually book a table in a good restaurant as a surprise, but he no longer wanted to. Why would he put effort into a marriage which had died years ago? Despite this, he didn't want to hurt Francesca because she deserved more. Was his behaviour already hurting her? It would destroy her if she discovered his affair with Michele, so why did he do it? The woman made him feel out of control, and he still returned for more! She was a mean irresistible woman, and they had a chemistry that he had never experienced with Francesca. Despite the incredible sex, he needed to get her out of his life before he ruined his marriage and reputation!

But how could he get rid of her when their offices were so close, plus there were the monthly network meetings? It was hard to cut her dead without embarrassing himself or alerting Adrian. It was a crucial time. He couldn't afford to let things slide when they were in the process of opening a new branch. He had planned to pay his staff more, but right now, what he needed most was loyalty. It wasn't easy to raise the staff wages; that was why he'd taken on a new Accountant to see where they could save money. Jade was certainly worth more. She was intelligent and sharp, and they paid her a pittance. If they didn't increase her wages soon, Jade would leave to work in a boutique or sell perfume. She was excellent at detecting aromas!

Brian looked at the conveyancing documents. Everything appeared in order apart from a small dispute over an adjoining parcel of land, but they couldn't exchange until they had identified the ownership. Conveyancing was such a headache when these things arose. Someone should have picked it up years ago, thought Brian as he finally confirmed the title number. He felt tired and walked into the reception area for some cold water to help him concentrate. He needed to check his messages, but he felt agitated and unable to focus.

Jade finished her call then said, 'Michele has called you five times. I said you were in a meeting and you're not available for the rest of the day. I hope I said the right thing?'

'Good, that's ok. I'm joining a conference call in a few minutes. Then I won't be available for the rest of the afternoon unless it's urgent.'

'If you don't mind me saying Brian, you look exhausted.'

'I've had to put in a lot of hours lately, Jade, preparing things for our new branch.'

'What new branch, will I be working there? Where is it?'

'Well, it's a bit hush-hush, Jade, but if it goes ahead, you will be the first to know.'

'I saw Michele at the Kizomba dance last week?'

'Michele?' answered Brian, who appeared dumbfounded.

'Yes, Michele, the lady who works at the accountant's, a few doors away. The woman who keeps calling you?'

'Really, you see her at what, Kizomba? Do you know her, Jade because she hasn't mentioned you to me?'

'No, I don't know her, but I saw her at the Kizomba night that I went to recently. That is another dance the salsa crowd do. She sat behind us, and she was drunk.'

'Are you sure it was her? I mean, I expect there are a lot of women who look like her?'

'No, Brian, it was her, I don't mean to be rude, but I've seen enough of her now to recognise her. I pass her every morning. I didn't talk to her because I wasn't sure, but I thought she looked familiar. She looked trolleyed!'

'Trolleyed?' What does that mean? She looked like a troll?'

'No, she didn't look like a troll, she was pissed, I was trying to be polite! It's none of my business, but I don't think she's doing you any favours. I thought I wore short dresses, but hers are long tops!'

Brian finished his water and threw the plastic cup into the bin next to the dispenser.

'Yes, she's bad news, Jade. I've got to get her out of my life before the shit hits the fan,' he muttered.

Jade didn't know what to say. She felt awkward, and it didn't feel appropriate to offer Brian advice. If he wanted to talk to her about it, then he would. Right now, she needed to think about her own life, but the number of times Michele had called the office over the last few days was unbelievable, she was becoming a pain!

Brian walked back to his office and closed the door. He then put his head on his desk, and ten minutes later, he was sound asleep. Jade could hear him snoring through the door, so she closed the Reception door and hoped the sound wouldn't carry through!

Oh dear, poor guy, Jade thought with a sudden wave of compassion. She'd have to say Mr Wilson was out for the rest of the afternoon. Hopefully, Brian would soon come to his senses and make it up with his wife. Jade was surprised to learn about them opening another branch. If that happened, then perhaps she would receive a promotion and decide to stay. Working as a shop assistant or cleaner could earn her more, but Jade liked working for the firm. Mr Tomlinson was friendly and polite, and she seldom spoke to him except to put an occasional call through, but she admired Brian's energy and enthusiasm and enjoyed his teasing! Even his comments about salsa had been humorous until today. Today felt different, and she hoped that she hadn't spoken out of turn by talking about Michele, but from what she'd gathered from people who knew her, Michele had a reputation! She came across as a hotshot accountant, but she enjoyed her drink. Jade had met women like her before, overpaid, oversexed and under danced. It was evident salsa would never be her thing because she didn't understand the basics. You should always give the man breathing space!

CHAPTER 8 – YOGA
CAMERON

It was now 1.30 pm, and Cameron had showered, changed and was ready for yoga with his light blue mat rolled up under his arm. He'd even watched a YouTube on yoga stretches. It had been a long time.

Sarah had previously warned Cameron if he joined a class, it was better to join the 6 pm class which some of the husbands attended, or he'd be the only man. But Cameron explained that he wanted to participate in the earlier lesson, so they could go to lunch and on to salsa! Sarah laughed. She knew that Cameron wouldn't turn up to her yoga class. Although he'd asked where it took place, he was jesting. He was an obvious flirt and joker who didn't take life seriously! Why would she have lunch with a man she had so little in common with apart from salsa? Yet, she couldn't deny that her mind had been on him since their last salsa class, and their recent kizomba dances were pure 'magic.' Cameron's charisma and magnetism had an unbelievable draw, along with the potential for real chemistry. But like anything hot, Sarah was worried that if she became involved, she would quickly burn!

There was a sudden hush in the room as Sarah put on some tranquil music. The ladies had already rolled out their mats, and they were sitting cross-legged on the floor. Sarah always gave her students five minutes of quiet time before the session started, followed by some gentle stretches. They were just about to begin when the outside door suddenly banged loudly, and her students jumped. Everyone looked up to see what was happening. The ladies usually ignored any noise from outside. But when the inside door flew open with a loud hi, their eyes fell on a good looking, muscular man with short, black dreadlocks and Cameron, who wore a loose black vest, joggers and white trainers, appeared ready to join the class.

Sarah breathed in deeply and tried to contain herself, then confidently said,

'Ah Cameron, please take a mat and join the class. Oh, I see you've brought your own.'

Cameron knew the ladies' eyes were on him, so he moved to the rear of the class and joined them in a cross-legged position. Sarah thought he looked very comfortable and at ease.

'This is Cameron. He's joining us today. He's a dancer,' she informed the class.

Cameron smiled and started to stretch. Sarah noticed her breathing had quickened, and she also became aware of the speed of her heart. Her class was usually calm and mindful, and Sarah wanted it to stay that way! So, she took some long deep breaths and decided not to give him any special attention unless he asked for help. When he tried to make eye contact, she found herself glancing down to avoid his gaze or checking around the room!

'We are going to do a balance now so touch the floor with your toe, then slowly lift your knee to stand on one leg. You can stand next to the wall if you need support. Even though the class had been doing this exercise for weeks, Sarah noticed that most of them still wobbled on one leg and they often placed their foot on the floor to start again. As she looked over at Cameron, she observed his balance was outstanding.

'That's very good, Cameron. You have great balance', she said.

Cameron smiled at her and something inside her melted. He chose not to reply, but he was listening to her instructions intently. He also appeared to find the exercises easy but was enjoying the class.

After an hour, they returned to their mats for relaxation, which always concluded the session. As Cameron laid back on his mat, Sarah noticed he was tall, fit, balanced, and radiated positive energy.

'Thank you for coming everyone. I'm sorry I won't be here next week because I'm going to France for a long weekend, but we'll be back the following week.'

As her students left, Sarah noticed Cameron waiting for her.

'I hope you enjoyed the class? To be honest, I didn't think yoga was your thing, but you got on well,' said Sarah.

'It most certainly is my thing. There are lots of things you don't know about me, Sarah.'

'Yes, I'm sure there are,' she replied, smiling.

'Are you ready for lunch?' he asked, then smiled broadly.

'Lunch, don't you think it's a bit late for that? You do realise it's after 3 pm!'

'Well, we can call it something else but either way, you promised that if I turned up, you would come, so, let's go, lady. We can have a drink in the town centre and then maybe try that Chinese buffet because they're open all afternoon.'

'Chinese buffet, no that will be far too heavy for me. I could eat a little vegan curry, something from the new Indian?'

'Vegan, well ok, but I don't know where that is so how about you take me in your car and drop me back later? I'll just put my mat in my car,' he said, sprinting over to his convertible.

Whatever he does for a living, he must be doing it well, thought Sarah looking at her ten-year-old mini.

Cameron jumped into the passenger seat, 'nice car,' he said.

'Nice but not flash', replied Sarah, who was slightly embarrassed by her humble offering.

'Flash isn't all it's cracked up to be. Simple and mindful are much more to my taste.'

Cameron turned his head to look into her eyes, and this time, Sarah allowed it. His head then quickly came forward to give her a small kiss on the lips.

'You're so perfect,' he said.

Sarah didn't know how to respond, so she started the ignition and pulled away slowly. She felt so excited her calm exterior had changed into a raging inferno! Could Cameron feel it? She needed a bucket of cold water to cool her down! As Sarah turned out of the community centre car park, Cameron started to squeeze her thigh just above the knee. She couldn't believe what he was doing and tried to focus on the road. Remain silent and just drive, Sarah thought, but she was beginning to lose control. Cameron had connected on so many different levels. There were no words to describe her feelings. She had been in complete denial because her heart said he was perfect too!

CHAPTER 9
SORRY HE'S IN A MEETING
MICHELE

Jade's afternoon had been busy. Thankfully there hadn't been any more calls from Michele, which was a relief and Brian had regained a few of his smiles. It was the first time in weeks that she had noticed her boss being light-hearted. He had also lost some weight which was probably due to all the strain he'd been under, but Jade thought he looked better for it.

Brian, who was now in his mid-forties, had a good head of blonde hair. He also had a fabulous physique because he worked out at the gym. He'd recently been taking longer lunch breaks so he could spend a decent time working out, which Jade thought worked well for him.

Jade tidied her desk. She had to leave things orderly for Maria, who was going to cover the reception this afternoon because her dentist appointment was at 3 pm and she wanted to purchase some more dance shoes before the trip to France. There was no way she could continue to dance in high heels which made her feet swell. It was going to be hot! Brian happily agreed and told her they weren't that busy so that Maria could cover. Jade seldom took time off, but as she was having a long weekend away, an extra couple of hours wouldn't make much difference!

Just as Jade was about to leave, a last-minute call came in. It crossed her mind to ignore it, but as she knew it was about a recent completion, she quickly answered it. She felt sorry for these people when things went wrong. They sometimes found their new house full of furniture, or they couldn't get hold of the keys to their new property. Despite hours of negotiations and all the paperwork complete, things could still go wrong, and Jade hated leaving people in the lurch.

After her check-up, Jade walked through the main shopping centre. It was now 3.20 pm, and the dance shop was open until 4 pm. She passed many bars and restaurants. There were newly renovated buildings, and there was now a Chinese, a new pizza place, and a new Indian restaurant.

As Jade walked past the restaurants, she peered through their windows. She had worked through her lunch hour today, and she now needed food. Jade had food at home in her fridge, so it was better to wait. Jade loved eating out, but all her late-night snacking had caused her to pile on the pounds, and she wanted to save money. With France being this weekend, eating out was a definite no if she wanted to fit in those dresses. Her phone beeped. It was Linda.

'Hi Jade, how many pairs of shoes and dresses are you taking to France? I'm stuck; I need to cut down on my clothes because I've got to squeeze them into a small case and be under the weight limit. I'm struggling! Have you got time to talk?'

Jade drew in her breath. 'I thought you had already paid for a large suitcase?'

'Well, I did, but I've decided that I don't want to carry anything that big the other end.'

Jade didn't feel in the mood for talking. She had answered seven hundred telephone calls today plus the last call, which was stressful, so the last thing she wanted to do right now was chat. After she'd visited the dance shop, she planned to go home, have a long soak in the bath and make a smoothie. By then, it would be time to get ready for salsa. So, she told Linda she was in a rush, and she'd talk to her later! She put her phone away and began to look at a menu affixed to the glass window of the new Indian restaurant. She decided there was no harm in looking. The vegetarian options were impressive. Perhaps a group of them could visit one evening after they'd returned from France. As Jade was still scanning the menus, she suddenly caught sight of Cameron sitting at a table close to the window with Sarah. Jade took another look. Perhaps she was jumping to conclusions. As she moved closer to the window, she saw Cameron point to the menu, as if to place an order. For a few moments, Jade stood still staring through the glass, completely mesmerised. She had been having regular sex with this man, and there he was with Sarah ordering a meal.

Jade felt shaky. She wasn't sure if it was fear or rage, but she continued to stare in disbelief. She wondered if she should walk in and surprise them, but what would she say? Had Cameron ever said they were in a relationship? She hastily walked away, feeling no longer capable of visiting the dance shop. Sarah had looked incredible, and she felt sick with envy. Well, Sarah always looked amazing, that was the problem. There was never an inch of fat showing, in whatever she wore, and her blonde hair tussled in indescribable ways. Jade suddenly hated Sarah, along with all the other perfect-looking girls! No wonder Cameron hasn't called, muttered Jade. He's dropped me like a hot cake!

Jade felt numb but decided to make her way home. She would make do with her heels because she was no longer in the mood to shop. As Jade began to walk, her whole body felt strange. She had lost her connection to the earth, and it felt horrible. But what did she see? Cameron was having a drink with a salsa friend. Why was that a problem? Once again, she heard Cameron's words. 'Don't tell anyone about us please because I'm not ready for that yet.' Even if they weren't in a relationship, he had been seeing her. Wasn't that the same? She felt confused and began to rush along the pavement at breakneck speed and quickly arrived home. Her feet ached. There were deep red marks on her heels, not again, she thought as she hurled her shoes in the kitchen bin. She then spread out on her sofa, put her head on a cushion and closed her eyes. She would make something to eat a little later because she wanted to dance. But how would she feel if she saw Cameron and Sarah together? Tears welled in her eyes as she began to sob. Everything was a mess. He'd fucked everything up, and now she didn't want to dance. Like he would care if she didn't go!

Jade's phone began to buzz. There was another message from Linda! 'Are you coming tonight?' Jade felt angry. 'Can't that woman leave me alone?' Linda was treating her like an emotional prop! Couldn't she decide anything on her own! Yeah, that was it wasn't it? She thought. I hold people up. I propped Linda up when she was down about Adrian, and I propped Cameron up by telling him how fantastic he was in bed, and soon if I'm not careful, it will happen with Brian. Well, the Jade prop has come down. How will they get on without me? She walked into the kitchen and took out some salad. Was it time to make a meal for a Princess? Jade cooked some pasta and chopped up a few fresh vegetables and created a delicious sauce. Whilst it was cooking, she decided to text Linda. It was better to send her a message now because she didn't want to chat!

'Sorry, I'm not coming tonight. I've had a hard day. I need to pamper myself!'

Linda had several dresses laid out on her bed. She had just selected a short midnight blue number when she received Jade's text. There was something wrong! Jade was a party girl who always came to salsa. It wouldn't be the same without her. She decided to leave it for now and talk to her on the way to France when they'd have more time, but her intuition said, Jade was distraught!

'Are you ok?' she messaged.

'Yes, I'm fine. I'm just looking after me.'

Linda put on some simple jewellery. If she wore anything dangly, it could fly up into the man's face, she thought, with a slight smirk! Linda couldn't wait until the weekend. She was so excited about having a long weekend on her own. Thankfully Adrian hadn't mentioned coming again, so Linda assumed his alternative plans were in place.

Half an hour later, Linda was on the dance floor dancing salsa with several different partners who were all excellent dancers. Every time Cameron met her eyes, she looked away from him. There was no point in engaging with him. They were over. It was better that he moved on to new pastures. It was a hard decision, but she planned to stick to it.

Her wine had just arrived at the bar when she suddenly noticed an unfamiliar woman standing next to her.

'Hi, I've not been to this class before. What's it like?' the slender dark-haired lady asked.

'It's good. I come most weeks, well I enjoy it,' Linda replied, smiling at the woman. She was beautiful and had the appearance of a sophisticated businesswoman. She thought she looked vaguely familiar, but she hadn't seen her at their club before.

'I normally dance crossbody. I don't know if I can get along with this Cuban thing where you keep rotating, but I'll try it because it looks fun. By the way, my name's Michele.'

'Michele, I'm Linda, pleased to meet you.'

'I usually dance at another club with my friend, but I thought I'd come here for a change. My friend's Receptionist, Jade comes here, and she told him it was fun.'

'Oh, right, well, Jade isn't here tonight, but she usually comes every week,' replied Linda.

The music changed to bachata. Linda quickly put down her drink because George had eagerly grabbed hold of her. He was sweating profusely. Linda kept a little distance between them and smiled at him as George quickly turned her back and forth in time with the music. His timing wasn't perfect, but he always tried and enjoyed himself. Linda was a little bored with the fact George never changed the routine, but if she kept a distance between them, she could tolerate him! She'd considered dropping a deodorant into his jacket pocket during a dance, but she was unsure how he'd react!

Michele was dancing closely with Cameron. She could undoubtedly dance the Bachata, thought Linda, feeling slightly miffed. As her head turned away from them, Linda suddenly caught a whiff from George's armpit. Fortunately, they were at the end of the dance, so she said thank you and hastily moved away. Where was Michele learning the Bachata, she wondered? They must teach other dances as well. The woman had talked to her as if she knew Jade, but Jade had never mentioned her. Strange, her perfume was lovely, though!

Linda suddenly turned around to see Cameron approaching her for the next dance. She thought about refusing him but, as the Kizomba beats echoed through the room, he gently took her hand to hold her close.

'Question my Heart,' by Kaysha was a song Linda wanted to forget, but Cameron smiled at her as they connected through the music, the lyrics spoke in a way that only they understood. Linda's heart knew that there would only ever be Cameron, but she didn't want to share him, and a small piece of him would never be enough. He had turned her world upside down without any word of commitment. When the music finished, Linda turned to walk away. Then she suddenly felt a crunch and realised she'd accidentally stuck her heel into the side of his foot. For one moment, she saw a look in his eyes, which replicated the pain she felt in her heart. It had happened entirely by accident, but it felt ironic.

'Sorry, was that your foot? I told you Kizomba wasn't my dance,' she said and forced an apologetic smile.

'Linda, you are good at everything. I would never be enough for you.'

Linda's mouth fell open for a but, then she quickly closed it again. She thought about her grown-up children, her husband and friends and realised that Cameron was right. He could never be part of her future. Their erotic novel was on the last page, and she had no choice but to add the words THE END.

CHAPTER 10
CAMERON

Cameron looked in the mirror. He'd been making more of an effort with his appearance lately and had even bought some shirts. He put one straight on from the packet. There wasn't time to iron when there was still a pile of clothes on his bed which needed packing. And he was still without a tent, but at this stage, it was easier to buy one in France. He'd enjoyed his meal with Sarah. She was strangely different, yet his attraction to her was intense. Maybe it was because she wasn't like the others, he wasn't sure. He didn't know if he could continue with her yoga class because taking time off work was difficult. If he could manage it, he'd go because there were benefits to being flexible.

He picked up his mobile. It had been quiet lately. Jade had hardly been in touch, which surprised him, and Linda appeared to have given up texting. He guessed she must have taken this 'it's the last time thing,' a bit too seriously! That was her all over. She was intense, but he'd loved being with her because she made him feel alive, well most of the time, when she wasn't fretting about her husband. Had the neighbours seen him, or could he please not do that! He always remembered his hat, but she reminded him about it every visit! It was better that he spent his time with someone single because he didn't want anything complicated. He liked Jade. She said the kindest things about his performance in bed, which made him laugh. He felt like a god and enjoyed appreciation, but Jade wanted more than he could offer.

Sarah had a different energy. Why had he started using that expression? His mates would think him a nutter! She was already rubbing off on him with her crazy talk. The girl put such a lot of time and effort into healthy eating and exercise that he wondered how she had the time for salsa! Perhaps she liked the company. That woman could dance, mostly when she wore those cute little shorts! Despite her crazy talk, he still wanted to spend time with her. He felt pulled, but at the same time, there was a small degree of resistance.

He looked in the mirror. The pattern hid the creases! It was grey with white palm trees, and had the eighties look! It accentuated his beautiful skin. He rubbed some oil into his palms and smoothed it over his dreads. He had to do something about getting them cut soon, or he'd be a ringer for Bob Marley!

He was glad Sarah was going to France, maybe they could share a tent. Why not, they were both single. There had to be a way to persuade her. He checked his watch because they were meeting for a quick drink at eight, so he would have to pack when he was home. The plane left very early in the morning, so he had to finish it tonight!

Cameron lived in a two-bedroom flat on the outskirts of Colchester. He liked his own space. He'd been in a relationship with Violet for what felt like a lifetime when things went wrong. She had suffocated him, and they argued most of the time. Whenever Cameron went out on his own, Violet complained. He had told her numerous times that he was a free spirit, but she never understood. When Antonne appeared, things snowballed. The sad thing was that he loved Antonne, but he preferred not to see him when it caused problems. He could take him out when he was older, besides what could he do with a two-year-old on his own? It was easier to get on with his life and wait and see what happened in the future. His parents were disappointed because they enjoyed being grandparents, but they had agreed to have Antonne over some Sundays. He sighed and chucked a deodorant into his hand luggage; it would save time later if he added a few things now. So long as he remembered his passport, money and dance shoes, he would be fine.

Working on building sites earned Cameron good money and allowed him a certain amount of flexibility. But his work was rapidly growing and taking time off to go on a trip at this stage was challenging.

It was already 7.45 pm, and Sarah wasn't the kind of girl to keep waiting. She seemed calm and cheerful, but she was busy. She had previously mentioned that her ex had annoyed her because he was inconsiderately late, so he didn't want to push his luck!

Cameron parked at the multi-storey, then quickly walked to a well-known wine bar just around the corner. As he arrived, there was no sign of Sarah, which was odd because she was someone who liked to arrive early! It was now five minutes past their arranged time, so Cameron pulled out his mobile to give her a quick call. He was slightly annoyed when it went straight to voicemail, so he decided to hang around for another five minutes, then leave. There was packing to finish. He also wanted to get to bed early. Cameron was unaccustomed to waiting for women, but Sarah was different because he wanted to see her. He was ready to leave when his phone buzzed, and a text came in.

Hi Cameron

'Sorry, I can't make it tonight. Something has come up, so please don't wait.

See you on the plane,' Sarah x

Cameron was annoyed and hungry. He hadn't eaten much all day, but life was too short for disappointment. At least she had bothered to let him know. Maybe now he could have his usual burger and chips with a couple of beers. They hadn't planned to eat, but if he'd eaten with Sarah, it would probably have been vegan! There was a place around the corner where he often went on a Friday evening, where there was never a wait for food, so he ordered a burger, chips and Guinness. Cameron thought about Jade. He hoped she wasn't going to cause a drama in France because he hadn't had the time to see her. Sarah said she saw her looking through the window into the Indian which wouldn't have helped. Perhaps she was wrong? There was something about Jade that reminded him of Violet. She wanted to please him all the time, then suddenly turned argumentative! Why couldn't women say no, in the first place if they were unhappy, surely the girl knew it was just sex. He took another swig of Guinness then noticed George standing at the other end of the bar in the business suit. It was the same suit he wore to salsa. Did he ever take it off!

George decided to come straight to the bar from work because it was the easiest way to find food since his wife had stopped cooking for him. He was trying his best to chat up a barmaid when he noticed Cameron at the other end of the bar.

George waved at him, and Cameron lifted his hand, but George's story about his unhappy marriage bored Cameron rigid, so he decided not to join him!

Cameron finished his beer and burger and left the bar. As he walked along the street, he noticed that the camping shop was still open. Cameron hadn't planned to buy a tent today, but it was worth a look. He'd walked past the shop hundreds of times, but he was surprised it was open this late.

'Are you closing?' he asked a very bored-looking young man who Cameron assumed would prefer to be out drinking with his friends on a Friday night.

'No, we're open until 9 pm,' said the young guy who appeared happy to have a customer.

'Ok, mate. Have you got a one-person tent?'

'Yes, they're over there. There is only one left. We've sold loads of them today because we're at the start of the festival season. Did you want a pop-up because I've got a few of them?'

'I don't care as long as it's for one person,' Cameron answered gruffly.

He picked up what appeared to be the last one which was surprisingly lightweight, and slung it over his shoulder.

'Going to a festival?' asked the sales assistant curiously.

'I'm going to a salsa festival, yes,' replied Cameron.

'Salsa? said the surprised young man. You can't do that in this tent. You can barely stand up!' he answered.

'That's when I salsa best,' said Cameron and strode off to pack.

CHAPTER 11
FRANCE

'Can I have a look in your case, Sir?'

Cameron forgot to set his alarm and had arrived late at the airport. There was no sign of the salsa group, so he assumed they had already gone through. Security was taking ages to check the cases, and there were five ahead of his. How long would they take? Cameron quickly checked his watch and muttered 'come on,' as he tried to focus on his breath, which was something he'd learned in Sarah's yoga class. 'Be mindful of your breath, particularly in stressful situations,' but how could he focus on anything when he felt so angry!

'Come on, mate. I've got to get this plane. It leaves in less than thirty minutes, and the gate is miles down the other end.'

'You should have thought of that when you left this morning, Sir,' said the security officer but to Cameron's relief, he then grabbed his case and searched it.

'It's all clear. You're good to go,' the man said, as he handed the case back to Cameron who angrily snatched it in haste.

'Thanks' he said, feeling aggrieved. He wanted to swear at him but thought better of it and began to run along the corridors to the gate. What was the number again? Ah yes, Gate 27.

As he approached the queue of people boarding the plane, he noticed the girls had begun to show their boarding passes to the airport staff. Cameron felt relieved that he had made it because he was the last person in the queue. He wiped the sweat from his brow and took off his jacket. It was way too warm for anything other than a tee-shirt. After he had pushed his luggage into the overhead compartment, he took his seat and smiled. It was incredible that he was on the plane when he thought he'd be on the next flight!

The buzz of conversation from further down the plane quickly drifted to Cameron's ears. He hoped the sound of the engines would soon drown out the noise because he needed to sleep! Jade's shrill voice was above the rest. She was talking about how excited she was, and how she'd been practising French. Ah, that's was why she didn't come to salsa, Cameron thought. He was surprised at missing Jade's warmth, but he didn't miss her mouth. If she gave up drinking, she wouldn't be as bad. Thank goodness he'd downloaded his favourite salsa tracks to his phone because it would eliminate any unwanted sound and help to pass the time.

As the plane took off, Cameron put his earphones in and started to drift into a light sleep. He was lucky that although he was one of the last to board, there was an empty seat next to him, which enabled him to spread out a little. He guessed that no one liked sitting over the wheels. Half an hour later, Cameron stirred. He'd completely forgotten where he was. He then realised he'd been dreaming about teaching salsa with Sarah! They had split the class into two groups. Sarah introduced the beginners, and he was leading the advanced level. He heard her counting one, two, three, five, six, seven as 'Devorame otra vez' played through his headphones. As Cameron stirred and stretched, he suddenly became aware of a soft leg resting against him, which caused him to wake.

'Hi, I'm sorry I didn't make it last night, but my mother fell over, and I had to rush over to help her. I didn't have time to explain by text. My Dad's away in Spain, and she called me as I was leaving to meet you,' explained Sarah apologetically.

'No, worries, you don't have to explain Sarah. I was in town anyway, so I decided to have a few beers, then I bought a tent!'

'Oh right, that's good. I've booked a Yurt because I need space to stretch and meditate. If I find things a bit noisy, then at least I'll have somewhere to relax.'

'A Yurt, what's that?' asked Cameron wondering if he'd missed out.

'It's a round building made of wood, and there's a hole in the middle for a wood burner. There are normally loads of mats inside. Yurts keep you warm in the winter and cool in the summer. The outside is canvas, a bit like a tent but round and bigger. You can fit quite a few people inside.'

'Oh, well, I can abandon my tiny popup and kip down in with you in this Yurt then!'

'No, I don't think so, Cameron. I've got it for yoga. I asked the organisers if I could put on some early morning classes. I'm going to do some free warm-ups for those who are interested.'

'I think they'll be too hungover from the night before to come to Yoga, but I'll try to come along because I enjoyed your class,' whispered Cameron as he leaned in close.

'Do you mind if I stay here because the others haven't stopped talking from the moment, we boarded the plane, and I want to listen to my music?' asked Sarah.

'Fine by me. As long as you don't expect me to talk because I'm listening to mine.'

Cameron put in his earphones and turned his head away to gaze out of the window. Sarah deserved a bit of a cold shoulder after last night. He didn't like excuses.

Sarah put in her earphones and opened her

book. She was halfway through 'A New Earth by Eckhart Tolle,' she had read it before but wanted a refresher. She was determined not to go into her shadow in any future relationships because her past experiences had taught her, it would cause conflict. Her inner child would demand attention, and Cameron's or whoever else she met would do the same. She had feelings for Cameron, but if anything was to develop between them, she wanted to remain present. Their chemistry was already so strong that Sarah could continuously feel it. She had learned that karmic relationships were magnetic and challenging, and they were also part of a healing process. It would be her choice to live out these unhealed issues with Cameron or to stop it in its tracks. But it was likely that if she avoided this lesson, her inner child would carry on screaming for attention and making her unhappy.

'What are you listening to?' she asked.

Cameron took his earphones out for a moment to look into her eyes.

The English Translation is 'Devour me Again'.

Sarah smiled at him and laughed, 'Devour, I only do tantra.'

'Tantra, what's that? Ah, yeah didn't Sting do something like that years ago where you sit opposite each other and meditate for hours before having sex?'

'Yes, something like that, but there is far

more to it than that. It's about remaining conscious and opening to something greater, God, the Universe, the Divine. It's about everything. Why we are here, co-creation, engaging in conscious relationships and sacred sex.'

Cameron looked at her for a moment, 'I think I'll stick to my one-person tent,' he whispered under his breath, putting his earphones back in. Fuck it, did he need it? She may be the hottest girl he'd ever set eyes on, and being vegan was a challenge, but this! Patience wasn't his thing. He liked moving on and fast because that's what he'd always done. It would take an exceptional woman to make him change that. He glanced over at Sarah, who was now quietly reading her book. 'A New Earth', what was wrong with the old one? After all, it had been around for millions of years and was doing ok. He smirked slightly and went back to his music because he knew the plane would be landing in Perpignan shortly and he was looking forward to the weekend now. These French girls were beautiful, and they were always short of male dancers so he would be in demand. Plus, they could all be wearing cute little shorts. It was hot.

Linda ordered a coffee and coke for Jade. It was costly, but she paid on her card. She felt relieved to finally be away from Adrian, where she could do as she pleased.

'To be honest, Jade, coming here was a lucky

escape. I had to tell Adrian that you'd been dating Cameron then you split up. You needed me to look after you because you were upset,' blurted Linda.

'Well, some of that's right because I am upset', replied Jade, who dissolved into tears.

'What? I didn't mean it, Jade, I was only joking. It was just a way of keeping Adrian at bay because he had invited himself along! Is there something you want to tell me?'

'Not really, it's just that, I did meet up with Cameron a few times, and we've been sleeping together.'

'What he fucked you? I can't believe that' Linda replied, with a horrified look on her face.

'Well believe it, Linda, because it's true. So, if you have also been, as you say, fucking him, I would appreciate you telling me.'

'No, Jade, I haven't been doing that. Cameron and I are soul mates, but I realised it was complicated, so we've parted company. I still have strong feelings for him, but I can't risk losing Adrian and my family; besides, I don't think he would ever fit into my life.'

'Why, because he's black?'

'No, don't be stupid, I'm not racist. Because Cameron hasn't been through the things I've been through and in some respect, we are worlds apart.'

'What makes you think that your soul mates then', hissed Jade, who was feeling a combination of hurt and anger and her voice had become louder.

'You just know, don't you?'

'But I don't know, do I, Linda because I've never met my soul mate! I just meet men who want to have sex with me. Even if I'm nice to them, they don't want to stick around or take me out on a date, although Cameron did take me for a pizza.'

'Where is he anyway?' asked Linda, who sensed the intensity of the situation.

'He's sitting further up the plane with Sarah,' replied Jade as she hastily wiped her tears. She then took out her makeup mirror to look at her eyes.

'Let's just ignore him,' whispered Linda. 'We don't have to dance with him. Let him find out what a cold shoulder is. I doubt Sarah's interested in him. She's far too sensible. Someone told me she teaches yoga and meditation. She isn't a casual type.'

'I don't know; I saw them together at that new Indian restaurant when I was walking home from work.'

'Really?' answered Linda, who quickly realised that she knew hardly anything about Cameron's recent movements.

The seat belt sign appeared, which indicated they would soon be landing. So, Cameron had been busy already! Did he go straight from her arms to Jade? Or had Cameron seen her at the same time? Surely, he wasn't that low, thought Linda, who suddenly felt furious. The man was despicable, and she had to put up with him all weekend!

As the plane's wheels hit the ground, they bounced slightly, and Jade gasped, but she was happy they were down because she hated flying. Linda just gazed out of the window. She could feel tears building up in the corner of her eyes, but she was determined not to cry in front of Jade. It was a shock that Cameron would go for her when he knew they were friends. Had she let go of this man? He was destroying her. Hopefully, this weekend would give her the chance to get him out of her system. Now that she was angry with him, it would be a lot easier. There would be loads of men to dance with, plus she could get by in French, so it was an ideal opportunity to move on.

Sarah looked up from her book and realised they had landed. She stood up, put on her sun hat, grabbed her case from the overhead compartment, and headed off without saying a word to anyone. She wanted to get through arrivals quickly and meet Jade and Linda on the bus to the campsite. With, a bit of luck by then, they would have finished discussing whatever they had been talking about the whole trip.

CHAPTER 12
ARGELES

The salsa group now consisted of Cameron, Linda, Jade, Sarah, George, Mark and Harriett, a young girl who dipped in and out of salsa because she worked in London. To everyone's surprise, Michele had also randomly joined them on the bus to the campsite. The site was three kilometres from Plage Du Racou and within reach of some other beautiful beaches. As soon as the group arrived, Linda discovered there was a bicycle hire for fifteen euros, which she thought worth doing. As they walked closer to the sign, Jade looked at her in disbelief!

'Linda, I haven't been on a bike for years, and it's a long way to cycle, even if the beach is excellent. Maybe I'll just stick around here and practice salsa moves in the marquee. Isn't there a bus to the beach, or a taxi we could share?'

'Jade this is the French Riviera. There are some incredible beaches plus a chance to mingle. We must explore, besides most of the dancing is in the evening so we'll have plenty of time during the day. Plage du Racou, Nice, Cannes, St. Tropez are all within easy reach, but we'll need to hire a car to reach some of them. Where have you been?'

'I've been working as a receptionist, Linda,' replied Jade. 'It may sound dull to you, but I enjoy it,' she replied, feeling a little put-down.

'I'm sorry, I didn't mean to criticise. There is nothing wrong with being a Receptionist! We're going to have great fun here, Jade. Hopefully, we'll receive some invites to a few beach parties; we'll see! I'm going to get my tent set up and then wander over to the bar for a gin and tonic a little later. I wonder if they have any cocktails? This site is amazing, it's so upmarket, and there's glamping. I think Sarah booked a Yurt, not that I know much about them. I helped to set one up once, but it took ages, and it was back-breaking.'

'I saw Sarah walk off in the other direction on her own. She wasn't with Cameron.'

Linda thought Jade sounded a little flat. She wished she hadn't pushed her to talk about Cameron on the plane. They had plenty of time to discuss what happened when they were back in England, and she didn't want to spoil their holiday.

'Can you forget about Cameron please, Jade? Remember we made a pact to ignore him. Let him get on with it; a cold shoulder is the best treatment for men like him. If I can do it, you can. Besides, there will be some great dancers here because salsa is extremely popular in France. You will be danced off your feet later.'

'Do they dance Cuban here?' asked Jade perking up.

'Yes, apparently, most of them dance our style. I looked it up before I came or it would have put me off. Well, that's it, my tent's up. I'll give you a hand with yours if you like? The ground is so hard. The pegs won't bang in far. I guess it's been hot here for a long time.'

'Does that matter? Do you think I'll get blown away in the middle of the night?'

'No, you won't get blown away. On the other hand, you might. It depends on who's here! There you are, it's finished. Now sort out your bed because I'm going to have a rest. I'll let you know when I'm ready to go for a drink.'

Linda went into her tent and zipped up her inner door to expose her mosquito net. She could see Cameron about twenty metres away, setting up his. He had revealed the lower part of his back. The back she had stroked and snuggled up to on many occasions, and Linda realised she still longed for him. The sight of him was painful. Even though it was baking hot, she then decided to zip up her outer door so she could no longer see him. Linda didn't want to see Sarah either. Later, she could have a few drinks to blot out her feelings. Hopefully, some of the other dancers would be a good distraction!

She let out a huge sigh! It had been fun hiring a blow-up mattress from the camping shop with Jade because the French word for a blow-up bed had been a little tricky, which led to a demonstration and a fit of giggles. Linda chuckled to herself. She was all over the place, either laughing or crying. It was time to move on, but it wasn't easy when Cameron was in her social circle. If she continued with dancing, he would still be around, so she needed to harden her heart!

Her phone buzzed, and a text appeared from Adrian. He had written it in French, which must have appealed to his sense of humour. She wondered if he was disappointed that he hadn't come on the trip? She felt mean, but she would have found him intolerable.

Salut Linda, J'espère que tu es bien arrivé. Vous avez oublié le lit gonflable, alors j'espère que le sol n'est pas trop dur. Peut-être pourrez-vous m'apprendre quelques mouvements de salsa à votre retour. J'espère que les français sont bons à ça? votre mari adorant Adrian

Linda smiled and felt a warmth of familiarity in her heart. The text said that Adrian was surprised she'd forgotten the inflatable bed and he hoped the ground wasn't hard. Maybe she could teach him some salsa moves when she got back! She often wondered whether Adrian would have been good at dancing, although if he rotated around a couple of movements like he had in bed, she'd rather not give him the opportunity!

Fifteen minutes later, Linda thought she was melting. The heat was stifling, and she hastily unzipped the door of her tent to allow in some air. As she looked across to the other campers, she noticed Sarah, standing outside Cameron's tent with what appeared to be two mugs.

'Probably tea, she thought, as Sarah doesn't drink alcohol. So bloody English!' she said out loud, venting her frustration. I wish that man would fuck off because it would make my life easier. She grabbed a book out of her case and stretched out on her mattress. Erotica no longer had the same appeal, so she'd bought the first book of a new detective series, and before she knew it; she was asleep.

Sarah also rested and awoke several hours later to the sound of crickets. She could smell the delicious soft scent of rain on the damp grass as she emerged with bare feet from the Yurt. She was happy that she'd booked it because it had already surpassed her expectations. There was plenty of room to sleep, stretch and meditate, and it would be quiet because it was a decent distance from the dance marquee. Cameron had stuck his head in earlier and noticed she had a kettle, but she didn't make them tea until after she'd stretched. She then took a mug over to his tent and then returned to her Yurt to sleep, realising the necessity to set her boundaries from the start. Hopefully, he understood that entering her space without permission wasn't an option. She knew that this weekend would be difficult because there was temptation everywhere. Opportunities for sex, alcohol and gossip were all around her which were pre-occupations she had worked hard to overcome.

Sarah's spirituality had been an individual journey, but she still craved the company of like-minded souls. When she took up salsa, she knew it would be fun, but vowed not to become 'involved', with the other dancers' lives, but this was proving to be more challenging than expected since her attraction to Cameron grew! Her only choice was to keep resisting him because if not, it could impact her social life. When Sarah danced, it balanced both her worlds, but she had to remain focused on what she wanted, a spiritual soulmate. A relationship where the man would have the emotional capacity to enter her world, and not be riding on a one-way train. Someone who wanted to build something great together. She knew Cameron had become attracted to her energy because it felt different. Was she different, though? Her body ached with desire for him, or was it the man she wanted him to be?

'Conditioned patterns, or egoic behaviours, one could say, don't go away immediately as you become present.' Sarah reminded herself. Eckhart was an incredible man who could quickly bring his wisdom to the fore; if only she could do that, it would solve all her problems.

Sarah tidied her things and closed the door to the yurt. There was a padlock on it, which was brilliant because it was secure. As she slowly walked over to the marquee, she noticed Harriett a little ahead of her. The young woman looked radiant. Her skin was a beautiful shade of ebony, and she wore a light pale orange cotton dress with a pair of sparkly gold sandals. Harriett quickly turned around when she heard Sarah walking behind her.

'Going to the bar?' she asked.

'I don't drink, but I'll come with you because we've still got a while before the dancing starts.'

'I hear you're giving yoga lessons tomorrow? I love yoga. I go to a class at Wimbledon, where I work as a nanny,' explained Harriett.

'Yes, I thought you did. I haven't seen you for ages. I didn't know you were coming to France with us.'

'I've been staying with my parents. I'm taking a few weeks holiday, so hopefully, I'll get to dance a bit more while I'm there.'

'Don't you dance in London?' asked Sarah.

'Yeah, I do, when there's time, but it's kind of full-on looking after a family.'

'I'd love to have children.'

'Believe me; there's no rush. If you worked with children, you might think twice.'

'Well, if I meet a decent man, it's a

possibility. I'm sure I'll have children eventually.'

'Yeah,' answered Harriett, who already appeared bored with their conversation! 'Are you going to keep drinking soda water or would you like to try Bacardi and coke? '

'No, as I said, I don't drink. I stick to soda water because it keeps my head clear and my dancing's better.'

Harriett ordered another Bacardi and didn't bother to order a drink for Sarah.

'What do you like the most about dancing?' asked Sarah.

'I don't know. I've been dancing since I was six. I started with ballet. Then I learned tap dance. Later I went to drama classes because I wanted to work in the Performing Arts, I still do.'

'Why don't you do that then, you still can?' replied Sarah, who suddenly became a lot more interested in Harriett. She had never really spoken to her before, but it was evident that the young woman was talented as well as beautiful. Her skin and eyes were so clear, and she radiated strong, irresistible energy.

'I had a boyfriend who put me off it,' she said quietly. 'He told me I was an average dancer and I wasn't a singer, so I decided to forget the whole thing. That's why I trained in childcare.' Harriett explained, despondently.

'Really. I think you're a Goddess. You know you can do whatever you want, but it takes determination and trust.'

'You make it sound simple. Do, you trust Sarah? I've never trusted men. I'm bi now, but I prefer women.'

'Yes, I do trust. I trust myself, and that's where it starts. I've always said relationships should be more about connection than gender.'

'I'm going to dance. I just saw Cameron walk into the dance tent. He's old, but he's a great dancer. He seems to have a harem of followers. Do you like him?'

'Yeah, he's cute. He's also got a great arse, don't you think?' said Sarah, who was shocked by how quickly her behaviour had changed!

'No,' replied Harriett, who quickly walked away in the direction of the music!

CHAPTER 13
JUST COOL OFF!

Linda awoke at 7.30 pm to the sound of loud music playing. She was amazed that she'd been asleep for nearly three hours which meant she'd have more energy to dance later! Her body was so hot that all Linda could think about was the feeling of cold water on her body. So, she hastily made her way to the shower block to cool off! It would be exciting tonight because she would, at last, be able to wear one of her new dresses and dancing with men, who spoke another language would make a complete change!

As she reached the shower block, Mark was leaving the men's toilets. He looked calm and relaxed in a white tee-shirt, pale blue jeans with a straw hat protecting him from the sun. Linda had always thought Mark would be more appealing if he didn't smoke because every time that she saw him, there was a cigarette hanging from his mouth. Smoking was so anti-social, and hardly anyone did it now. Why couldn't he use a vape thing, which was marginally better than exhaling fumes over people!

'Hi, you look nice and cool. Have you seen Jade walk this way because she isn't in her tent?' asked Linda as she forced a smile.

'Jade, who's she? Oh, you mean that chubby blonde with the heels and nice legs,' replied Mark, chuckling to himself.

'Well, you could describe her like that, but it's rather mean. She's in the tent next to mine. I've tried calling her and texting, but there's no answer.'

'Perhaps she's busy! I heard a couple of people in the ladies earlier, making a lot of noise while I was taking a shower. You know, grunting.'

'Don't be disgusting, Mark, I'm sure that wasn't Jade. Was it in the ladies or the men's?

'I said the ladies, you were probably asleep, so were most of the other dancers after their journey here. It's so hot.'

Mark suddenly appeared edgy. Linda knew that he'd taken too many drugs in his time which had wrecked his nerves. Mark still smoked cannabis and, was often sarcastic. Then he wondered why she didn't bother to chat! Mark enjoyed being crude, probably due to working in those sleazy London clubs for too many years. Most of the dancers avoided talking to him because they found him unpleasant.

Linda breathed and pulled in her stomach. She'd been putting on a bit of weight lately, and most of her clothes were tight. Perhaps it was another menopausal symptom or just an age thing? She frequently got away with telling people she was 42, and they believed her, but she didn't feel forty-two. Recently she felt sixty, especially when she couldn't keep her eyes open between 3 and 4 pm!

Linda gave up on Jade and walked into the surprisingly clean showers. As she went into the first cubicle, she noticed something sparkling in the plug hole and bent down to pick it up. It shone in her hand. It looked familiar then she realised it was one of Jade's earrings. One of the pair she had worn on the plane. Jade had loads of earrings but had treated herself to some dangly ones at the airport. She still had them on when she went through the scanner and had set it off! So, Jade had dropped an earring in the shower, that didn't mean a thing.

Linda washed and dried her hair. Then applied her makeup, put on her evening dress and added some carefully selected jewellery. It was a lot easier getting ready in the showers than in her tiny tent! Half an hour passed, and there was still no sign of Jade, so Linda decided as she wasn't her mother, she would get a drink and enjoy herself.

A few minutes later, Linda walked into the marquee to find Jade, Cameron and Sarah all talking together like old pals. Mark, Harriett and George were already dancing. Michele was talking to a couple of French guys with what looked like a gin and tonic. At least Linda thought they were French because she could just make out their accents.

'Hey Linda, where've you been?' asked Jade, who had turned around to include her in the conversation.

'Oh, I had a long sleep. I slept for three hours; would you believe it? I was exhausted. I found this in the shower Jade. I think it's your new earing?'

'Ah yes, thanks, Linda, I wondered what happened to that. I should have the other one somewhere?' she replied as she put it in her ear.

Sarah smiled at them, then walked to the bar.

'Un citron vert et soda s'il vous plaît' she said, in her best French accent.

A tall, dark-haired man suddenly walked across the dance floor to join her and gently took her hand. Sarah was surprised that the French man was confident enough to approach her while she was still at the bar!

'Bonsoir, voudriez-vous danser?' he said, which Sarah assumed was an invitation to dance. She hastily paid for the drink then took the man's eager hand, which surprisingly felt like velvet to the touch. Sarah very quickly fell into rhythm with his unique style of dance. He danced Cuban, but he also led her into some unfamiliar steps which she managed to follow by keeping aware of his subtle leads, which she felt through her body.

'Are you the lady who's teaching yoga tomorrow?' he asked in English. I'm a yoga teacher. I want to join you. What time is the start?'

'Just come along at 7 a.m.,' Sarah replied. She had begun to feel enchanted as they continued to dance with ease. She noticed the young man was beaming at her.

'Merci, vous êtes une belle danseuse' he said, which Sarah understood was thank you, you are a beautiful dancer.

Sarah looked at the attractive man and smiled, realising, it was a compliment. She had received many compliments about her yoga, but having someone say she was a beautiful dancer, made her light up.

The music moved onto Bachata, and Cameron quickly took her hand.

'What did he say?' Cameron asked.

'He said he was called Andre and that he taught Yoga. He wants to join my group tomorrow,' explained Sarah.

'Ah ok,' he replied, realising the necessity to move fast to keep her attention. Cameron had observed there was an abundance of good-looking French men for the ladies to dance with, who were unexpected competition! He sadly lacked basic French so if he wanted to communicate with a French girl, his only choice was to take her hand and pull her towards him, and he wasn't sure how well that would go down! Perhaps he could learn a few words by googling them on his phone. It couldn't be that difficult!

'What are you doing tomorrow, Sarah? I thought I'd cycle to the beach if you'd like to join me? Maybe we could take a picnic or have a beach BBQ?' Cameron said as he looked into her eyes.

'Yes, that sounds good. We could invite Jade and Linda, so there is a group of us. I want to go to Cannes, but I hear this beach at Ville Franche Plage is stunning. We can go anywhere if it's cycling distance. I've wanted to come to the South of France for years. There are so many beautiful beaches here. I love dancing, but I want to see as much as possible while I'm here,' replied Sarah, who was amazed at Cameron's sudden eye contact.

'Ditto', said Cameron smiling. 'Cannes is a long way, though, so we'd have to hire a car between us.'

'You're out of time?' Sarah remarked.

'No, I'm never out of time, so you must be drunk on lime and soda!' he replied candidly.

Cameron looked disgruntled and decided to dance with a French girl who he soon discovered was very happy to accommodate his pull her method of approach! It was becoming hot, and there was an array of available women. He didn't need to dance with Sarah or any of their group if they were going to be hard work, but Sarah had got under his skin, and he had to find a way to keep her attention!

CHAPTER 14

EXTREMELY FRAGILE - JADE

Jade walked off the dance floor and out of the marquee to cool off. The evening air was hot, but at least it was colder than the air inside the marquee, which resembled a sauna. After eight salsas, three bachata's and two kizomba's Jade had lost count of her dances. She just kept going and going, but now her feet hurt. Despite having some great dances, she felt an emotional emptiness which was hard to put her finger on, plus, the other earring was still missing! Linda had returned one, but where was the other? Had Cameron picked it up, or had it disappeared down the plughole?

The incident in the showers happened so fast Jade didn't have time to think. Cameron, who was naked, had suddenly appeared behind her. They seemed to be the only ones in there. Had he known that? Perhaps he had followed her inside? The more her mind went over it, the angrier she became, especially since Linda had revealed her affair! How many women had Cameron had? She had to draw a line and move on, but she found him hard to resist! It hadn't helped when he called her beautiful because no one had said that. But he hadn't said anything like that in the showers. The sex had been fast, demanding and uncomfortable!

Jade was worried about her reputation. How many people could have heard them, not everyone was sleeping! They had been noisy and, even with the water running, anyone passing by would have wondered what they were doing? As soon as she saw Cameron's wet toned body, she gave way to her desires, but the thought of it now made her feel sick. She also felt ignored because he hadn't asked her for a single dance this evening. It was painful and worst still she had broken her pact with Linda, the friend who looked out for her, God, life sucked!

Jade removed her dance shoes. Her feet had doubled in size due to the heat and excessive dancing! She wondered how on earth they would go back on because she couldn't dance barefooted when everyone was going wild! She walked off the dance floor and into the bar to order a vodka, being careful that no one trod on her toes. She couldn't see where the group had gone, but her friends had slung their jackets and cardigans over some nearby chairs. She knocked back a double vodka and decided to go back to her tent. It wasn't as if anyone would miss her, certainly not Cameron. Jade's head was spinning. She wanted to cry. What happened to Michele, the woman who had hounded Brian, she wondered. She could do with a nice man like him. It was tough that all the good guys were married. Michele hadn't talked to her yet because she always had a group of men around her. Jade hadn't seen her dance much either. She'd check on Michele tomorrow. It was brave of her to come to the weekender on her own. She looked stunning in short dresses with her lovely slim thighs. Maybe that was what Brian liked, skinny women in tiny dresses!

Jade lifted her dress and looked down at her legs. She knew they were fat, and she hated the sight of her thighs, it upset her. Cameron had lied about her being beautiful. He wanted to shag her. She had stopped having casual sex five years ago, but that horrible man had managed to pull her back into it! If he tried again, she'd tell him to fuck off because he'd made her feel like an idiot!

The zip to Jade's tent appeared to be stuck, and she struggled to open it. To her relief, it eventually opened. She then hurled herself inside and crawled along the ground to her sleeping bag. Her favourite salsa track had started to play. Sting sang 'Fragile,' in a way that completely resonated with her and she immediately noticed the lyrics. The words depicted her feelings, and she wasn't sure whether to dance or howl! Jade wondered about going back to the Marquee, but as she tried to stand, she lost her balance and collapsed down on her bed. Jade felt frustrated, lost and alone. When there was no dry place to rest her head, she turned over her pillow, and eventually found sleep. Her world had turned into a cruel place where rejection was rife, and her future uncertain.

* * * * * * * * *

Several hours later, Jade woke up to discover she was in an uncomfortable pool of sweat. Her legs were stuck to her sleeping bag. It was shortly before seven, and the sun shone through the tent walls making the inside a crazy temperature! She slowly stretched her arm out to reach a bottle of water, which was also hot and groaned. Her head still pounded from last night's alcohol. What happened? Why did she leave the dancing so early? She was on holiday. The idea of coming on this weekend was to dance and to have fun!

Jade noticed last night's puffiness had disappeared from her feet! Wow, there was something positive, she thought as she wriggled her bottom to the edge of her bed. Standing was still tricky because her body wanted to flop down. Why was she awake so early? Had her alarm gone off or something? Jade quickly stripped off her clothes into her bra and knickers and lay on the top of what resembled her air bed to gather her thoughts.

'Jade, are you in there? Are you coming to yoga? I don't want to go on my own. We've only got five minutes before it starts,' shouted Linda enthusiastically.

Oh, that was it, yoga. 'You must be kidding', Jade mumbled. 'Being on holiday with you is worse than being at work,' she shouted, staggering to her feet. Her head and body remained bent while she searched for her towel and sponge bag. Five minutes or not, Linda would have to go on her own because it was shower time!

'Ah, there you are?' shouted Linda as Jade emerged. 'We looked everywhere for you last night, but you had disappeared. I was going to call you, but someone said they saw you go back to your tent, so I guessed you weren't in the mood to party?'

Linda had already dressed in denim shorts and a tee-shirt with,' Vive La France' printed on the front. Jade thought she appeared very bright and breezy so early in the morning!

'I don't do yoga, Linda. I can't get into the positions. I'm not flexible enough. We're not all bendy like you!'

'Come on, Jade, it will be a laugh. You don't have to do the whole class, Sarah assured me it was a few simple stretches, plus we can have a nosey at the Yurt. Cameron said there was a kettle, and I could do with a strong coffee.' she continued loudly.

'Oh, so you spoke to him? Can you whisper please, Linda, you're very loud! Alright, I will come, but I must take a shower cos look at me, I'm still dripping from last night. I slept in my clothes. I was too tired and pissed to undress. I went to yoga years ago, but I can only do that doggy thing, and that's when I'm not hungover!'

'You mean downward dog, that's quite advanced. Look take a hankie, I bought some to wipe the sweat off. I knew it would be hot.'

'Aren't they for men?' Jade replied, gratefully taking one.

'No, of course not,' replied Linda placing one in her back pocket. These hankies are for women. I got them in our favourite store. You'll be ok but don't mention that doggy thing because it won't do you any favours.'

Jade chuckled and headed towards the showers. This time she'd be quick. She felt more upbeat about the yoga class, and besides, the Yurt sounded interesting, so she decided to give it a go.'

Sarah was in a great mood. She had woken at six, stretched and was looking forward to her breakfast after the class. If there were more than six of them, the yoga would be on the grass. There was a pile of mats in the yurt which they could use. By 7.15 a.m., she was amazed to see quite a few of the dancers had turned up apart from Jade, who was going to be late, so she decided to make a start.

'Hello everyone, thanks for getting up so early. I'm going to teach you a few balances which will help your dancing, but first, stand with your feet shoulder-width apart and breathe in slowly, count to four, then release. Then imagine roots coming from your feet down into mother earth. Try to release anything don't want to hold on to,' continued Sarah looking at the group.

It wasn't long before everyone was enjoying their yoga stretches. They were smiling and laughing at each other as they complained about their lack of flexibility. Sarah was very understanding, and she walked around the group, helping them individually with the utmost patience. She had made it clear that it wasn't a good idea to overdo it. Jade quickly joined the class and found that even she was more flexible when she relaxed. Linda found it easy, and Harriett who had done yoga before was in a class of her own!

The Frenchman arrived ten minutes late but was still keen to join in.

'Bonjour Sarah, Je suis désolé, je suis un peu en retard, mais j'ai bien aimé danser hier soir et les Français apprécient leur vin!'

'What did he say?' asked Jade, nudging Linda. She had just arrived and felt fresher. She perked up even more at the sight of the attractive

Frenchman.

'He said, he's sorry he's late. He enjoyed last night's dancing but the French like their wine!' said Linda. Well, something like that, we can look it up later. We need to stay focused and concentrate on our breathing. Relax your shoulders, Jade. You look tense.'

Jade suddenly felt upset. She knew standing on one leg would be hard because her balance was terrible, plus if she let go, the flood gates would open. After a few attempts at various exercises, she decided to tell Sarah she couldn't do it.

'I've tried, but I've had enough now, Sarah, so I'll see you later,' she announced, walking away.

'That's fine, Jade. Releasing is like peeling back a layer of an onion. That layer might not be ready to come off yet. Why don't you just sit and watch for a while, we should never force things. Release happens when we are ready.'

Jade sat down on a brightly coloured mat with her legs outstretched enjoying the sun. It was a beautiful day, and she couldn't wait to go down to the beach, even if it meant putting her body through more pain, cycling!

Sarah resembled a graceful, majestic swan that glided with ease into different poses. Linda had a couple of wobbly attempts before she too stood gracefully on one leg. Jade sat there and watched them with interest. Sarah then started to talk about the left and the right sides of the brain, which Jade found annoying, so she took out her phone and noticed a text from Michele.

'Hi Jade, do you want to meet later? I feel a bit left out here because I don't know anyone. What are you doing?'

Jade decided to reply because ignoring her felt mean.

'Hi Michele, how did you find my number? I'm in a yoga class right now, but we're going to the beach this afternoon to Rueda. We're meeting outside the bike hire at 2 pm so see you there?'

'Great', she replied.

Jade took a long deep breath. She wondered why she always had to please others instead of looking after herself. She didn't even like Michele, so why did she invite her?

* * * * * * *

At 2 pm, the group assembled around the bike hire when Linda suddenly noticed Cameron was absent. He should be here by now, she thought despondently.

'Where's Cameron?' she asked the rest of the group.

'I don't know, I haven't seen him since yoga this morning, has anyone else?' replied Sarah.

'No, sorry I don't know, but I don't think we should bother waiting, because I want to get to the beach,' answered Jade, who felt relieved.

'I'll text him, perhaps he's fallen to sleep or something?' said Sarah, as she took out her mobile.

George arrived. He looked sweaty and out of breath because he had been running.

'I'm so bloody hot. Still, with weather like this, I can take my shirt off.

The group watched George as he stripped off to reveal a white hairy upper body which rippled as he moved.

'Maybe you should keep that covered because with fair skin like yours; you'll fry in about half an hour, suggested Linda tactfully.'

'Fry, you mean burn? Ok, I'll wear a tee shirt and put this back because it's my favourite. I didn't bring many clothes. Julie is tired of washing and ironing, so I do it. But there's not much time when I'm stuck at the office.'

'Well, you're not in the office now, are you? There's a laundrette behind those toilets over there if you want to wash anything George. You must buy soap powder. Have you seen Cameron because we've been waiting over fifteen minutes and we want to go to the beach? We have to return the bikes by 6 pm?'

'Cameron, oh he's gone,' answered George.

'What do you mean, he's gone?' replied Linda, unable to hide her disappointment.

'I don't know why he left. He sent me a text about ten minutes ago. He needed to go home because something's happened. I saw a taxi come, so I guess he took a flight back to England.'

Linda, Jade and Sarah all looked at each other in amazement.

'Good', said Jade.

'What do you mean good, that isn't very nice,' answered Sarah in a slightly raised voice.

'Well, that man's an energy-sucking vampire who uses and abuses people, and now he's gone, we might be able to get on and have some fun! Cold shoulder, eh, Linda?'

'I need to meditate. I can feel a drop in my energy,' whispered Sarah.

'So, you're not coming either?' that sucks, replied Linda.

'I'll meet you on the beach later, in about an hour or so. I just need some space to rebalance.'

'What, after all that yoga?' asked Jade.

The group grabbed their bikes and started to pedal. They were all there now, including Michele. They were keen to try Rueda on the beach. Andre, the French yoga instructor, asked Linda if he could join them.

'Yes, of course, we need more male dancers because they are dropping like flies,' she replied.

'Dropping like flies,' said Andre, looking puzzled.

'Oh, never mind,' she said, smiling.

Linda realised she'd have to brush up on her French conversation to converse with Andre. She had already become attracted to him during their incredible dances, and she wanted to single him out, but he needed to understand her!

Sarah returned to the yurt. How could Cameron leave? It was unbelievable! If she had known this was going to happen, she wouldn't have bothered to come. It was already challenging coping with Linda and Jade when they had a problem with him. She had to centre and raise her energy to let this go because but it kept nagging at her. She hated secrets, but equally, she didn't want to be involved.

Five minutes later, Sarah sat crossed-legged on a mat in the middle of the Yurt and breathed deeply. She'd turned off her mobile phone because the more she connected to it, the worse she felt. Cycling to the beach alone would be great because the beautiful scenery would ground her. It was anti-social not to join the others, but she couldn't put up with that talk!

'Shit,' she said out loud, as tears ran down her face, 'I've fallen for him, after all, I did to prevent it.'

Let it out Sarah said a knowing voice in her head. You need to release. You are human, so why do you always give yourself a hard time? You just love that stick, don't you, the one that beats you up and tells you that you don't need anyone or anything. This perfection is isolating you. You can't communicate with others because you don't listen to yourself. You need to relax and experience fun and joy.'

Sarah's mind drifted into a relaxed state. She experienced a completely changed reality by connecting to her spiritual self. As she went deep within, she let go of judgement, not only of others but of herself. Sarah had been meditating for about fifteen minutes when she laid back on the mat to embrace her new realisation. As she watched the shafts of sunlight stream through the open doorway, she observed Cameron standing in complete silence, and she blinked to see if he was real.

'What, you're still here? I thought you'd left ages ago?' she said, in surprise.

'No, I was leaving, but I've managed to sort it. I won't go into it. Can I come in please, or is this Yurt a member-only club? I didn't want to make you jump, so I waited until you opened your eyes. You looked very peaceful' he said softly.

'It's ok Cameron, come in if you like. Shall I make us some tea?'

'Well, what've you got,' he replied, jestingly.

'Nettle?'

'Well, nettle it is then, although I'm not used to nature's divine substances.'

'Really?' Well, if you don't try them, you never know how amazing they are!'

Sarah filled the kettle and turned on the gas.

She thought Cameron appeared very calm as he slowly sat down on a mat to face her. He then carefully removed his trainers.

'I've been reading a book on tantra, which I downloaded to my phone. It seems a bit long-winded, but I understand how important it is to have a connection with someone before engaging in sex. Sex can be sacred and transformational if the two people are of like mind.'

'Yes, well something like that. We all see things from different perspectives. That is the joy of being human, people are always in a hurry, but I guess if we didn't have movement, we would still be waiting for the wheel,' she said then started to laugh. 'But seriously I think we have forgotten how to be still and we need to relearn it

'The kettle's boiling. Shall I make the tea?' asked Cameron.

'Yeah, why not?' Sarah replied, who found she had eased up after their laughter.

'I'm bloody boiling, aren't you?' She continued, suddenly stripping off her tee-shirt to reveal a small lacy bra.

'Is this Tantra?' asked Cameron, who then removed his hat, which allowed his dreads to drop down to his shoulders.

'No, I'm just hot,' she said, pushing Cameron to the ground. 'God, I want to fuck you. Do you mind if I take charge because I have a dominance problem?'

'Don't mind me, I love it, but do you think we should shut the door?' asked Cameron as he stared at Sarah in disbelief.

'No, we'll get too hot, and the dancers are at the beach. Besides, we may need a breeze.'

A few minutes later, Cameron confidently turned Sarah on to her side to continue their lovemaking, Vegan or not. This woman was most certainly his type. She's fit, thought Cameron. He enjoyed Sarah's dominance, which brought out a new side of his masculinity, and Sarah forgot about her search for the ideal man and started to enjoy herself! Despite the hard ground, the earth supported their bodies and celebrated their combined energies. Sarah knew it wasn't tantra, but it was more than lust!

As they lay side by side, looking up at the roof of the unique little building, Cameron told her she was beautiful.

'And you are a God,' Sarah whispered.

'You make me feel like a God, but I don't have the powers of one,' he replied.

Sarah laughed. She wasn't going to explain about creating your reality because it would take forever, and she had enjoyed what they shared.

'Shall we go and join the others?' she asked, becoming aware of her promise to meet the others.

'Yes, but we don't have to go just yet, do we? Can I have some more of that tea because it's a magic potion?'

'Oh, the nettle! I made it this morning. There are loads of them around the back of the Yurt', she replied.

'Are you trying to sting me, Sarah? First all this tantra talk and now the nettles!'

Sarah had forgotten how great it was to laugh. She was amazed at how light she felt in this man's company. Perhaps now, she could smile more often because Cameron had awoken something which had laid dormant for far too long.

CHAPTER 15
RUEDA

Cameron and Sarah left the campsite and were soon cycling along long leafy lanes on their way to the beach. Breath-taking scenery surrounded them, and they gazed at the views of the distant mountains. When they stopped to ask for directions, the French people, they encountered appeared friendly, but Cameron left all the communication to Sarah, who appeared to be good at French!

'You're good at French, and you are fast on that bike,' shouted Cameron, who was struggling to keep up!

'I've got a bike at home. It's a bit of an old one, but it works well. I cycle to my yoga classes. It's better than taking my car out all the time,' Sarah replied. The pair were now cycling side by side, so Sarah kept her eye out for traffic, even though the country lanes appeared quiet.

'You Eco-Warrior you! Do you think they've started the Rueda already because I wanted to call?' asked Cameron.

'Probably, they would have started ages ago because it's nearly four. I'm not sure if they will manage to dance on the beach, but there are some large concrete areas they can use, that will draw the crowds! I looked at some pictures of the beach early this morning on the internet.'

As they arrived, they immediately noticed George had organised the group of dancers on an area of concrete along the seafront. The little Taverners on the beach were full, and some of the people clapped at the dancers.

'Look at that! Watch George go! What an incredible beach. Look at that beautiful sand! The sea looks amazing and wow, look at the view of the mountains. This place is awesome.' Sarah said. She suddenly felt excited and wanted to run down to the sea like a child.

'Let's just sit on the beach and watch for a bit because they are right in the middle now. Hopefully, I can call the next one,' said Cameron, who hadn't given up the idea of calling.

'Yeah, it will be good to watch instead because there are still a lot of steps, I don't know in Rueda. It's so fast you don't have the chance to think. I'm usually swinging around at a hundred miles an hour.'

'If I swung you around at a hundred miles an hour, it would distort your face,' joked Cameron as he stuck his tongue out to make a strange face! 'I'm too hot with my jeans on. I don't know why I'm still wearing them because I'm wearing trunks underneath.'

'It's baking. I have my bikini on under my shorts too, but I think I will get changed after the dancing because I want to watch.'

Cameron stood up and wrestled out of his jeans, which appeared tight with his swimming shorts underneath. Sarah was surprised that he'd managed to cycle so far wearing both!

'The view here is breath-taking. Mountains surround us, and the sea is the bluest shade I've ever seen,' said Sarah, who was trying not to look at Cameron when his shorts slipped down with his jeans!

'Stunning, a bit like you,' he replied as he gave her a gentle kiss.

Sarah eagerly returned Cameron's kiss. She had been reflecting on how quickly they had come together after he had supposedly gone home!

'I bet you say that to all the dancers', she said, giving him a light punch.

'You may think that Sarah but I don't have relationships with any dancers. I haven't been with anyone for a long time. I may appear to be a flirt, but I do enjoy my own company, and it would take a special kind of woman to attract my attention.'

'Am I special then?'

'I don't need to answer that question, or I wouldn't have looked for you in the Yurt.'

Sarah smiled. It was blissful sitting in the sun

with Cameron, but she felt the need to join in the dancing and stood up.

'Come on then, let's go over because we're missing all the fun.'

As Cameron threw his jeans over his arm, Sarah suddenly noticed something glistening in the sand.

'What's that?'

'I don't know, but leave it because whoever lost it will come back.'

'No, I better pick it up because it could belong to a dancer,' replied Sarah picking up the glistening object, which on closer inspection was an earring.

'This looks like Jade's earring. I remember she was only wearing one last night, and I asked her why? She told me that she'd lost the other one in the showers. Did it fall out of your pocket? What are you doing with her earring?'

'Let's go and dance. I've never seen it before. Let's leave it on the beach. Come on; we need to go.'

'Oh, do we?' shouted Sarah, who suddenly felt annoyed.

Sarah walked over to the group and took her place in the circle. She stood between Linda who was dancing with Andre, Jade and Mark.

'Hi Sarah, I didn't think you were coming, but I'm glad you're here because we're short of women! Are you on your own, or is Cameron with you? We thought he'd gone back to

England?' whispered Linda.

'It's complicated. I think Cameron's watching. Jade, is this the earring you lost in the showers?'

'Wow, thanks, where did you find it? I've been looking for it everywhere.'

'I didn't find it. It dropped out of Cameron's pocket. I'm not going to ask why he had it! Can I call please George because I speak Spanish, and I need some fun?'

'Yeah, go ahead, Sarah, it will give me a break, and I want to dance now,' puffed George as he joined the circle.

Sarah stood at the front of the group and began to call. The sun was unbelievably hot, but there was a gentle breeze that took the edge off. She was pleased she'd applied suntan lotion to her legs because she was wearing her very short denim shorts!

She noticed Cameron some distance away, sitting on a bench. She thought it was easier to ignore him and focus on the dance. If he came any closer, she might lose her temper and slap him. How many women had he had?

'Right,' she said, then took a long deep breath before starting!

'Dile que no,' she began, suddenly realising this was harder than envisaged, without a list of names in front of her. Still, she forced herself to carry on, 'Exhibela.' Sarah noticed that everyone was responding well, so she continued with a few more bold moves. 'Enchufla', Enchufla p'al medio con dos and she was relieved that everyone was dancing and clapping in time.

Cameron suddenly appeared next to her.

'Can I help?' he asked.

'No, I've got it covered, thanks. Guapea, now dile que no, move on,' she called as more steps came flooding back to her.

Cameron sat down on a nearby bench that overlooked the group. Sarah thought he was waiting for her to finish, but he looked at his watch and walked off in the opposite direction.

'Where did he go?' asked an out of breath, Linda, as they finished the dance.

'I've no fucking idea,' replied Sarah, 'maybe he's gone back to England, after all.'

'God, you're angry, that's not like you. What happened to the calm and centred bit?'

'Well, I'm still human despite my spiritual teachings,' blurted Sarah, who was on the edge of tears.

'Oh, please don't tell me he had you as well?' replied Linda, looking at her intently.

'I don't want to talk about it, but all I'll say is this, he puts on a compelling show.'

'What are we going to do now?' asked Jade taking a swig of water. 'It's far too hot to dance, and we don't have long before we need to return the bikes.'

'I'm going down to the sea, would anyone else like to join me?' Sarah said confidently.

'I'm coming,' replied Jade, who stripped off her shorts to reveal a fancy bathing suit, and started running towards the water. She felt exhilarated by the opportunity to bathe in such beautiful surroundings.

'It's so warm. It's fantastic! Just like a warm bath,' exclaimed Linda, who began to float on her back.

'Yes, it will wash away the debris,' shouted Sarah.

'You mean the fallout?' replied Linda.

'Whatever you call it, toxic waste? Let's not fall out with each other over this. We may all have known him, but us girls have to stick together,' declared Sarah.

'Soul Sisters?' announced Jade.

'Ok, agreed. I think Cameron is going to be short of dance partners,' replied Sarah, who had perked up a bit!

'I don't know; he still has plenty of admirers. What about that young girl who's always dancing with him?' asked Jade.

'You mean, Harriett,' said Sarah.

'Yeah, Harriet, I forgot her name.'

'Harriett's bisexual. She's got a girlfriend in London,' explained Sarah.

An hour later, Sarah, Linda and Jade had dressed and were cycling back to the campsite. They appeared to have split from the rest of the group and had bonded into a group of their own, which Sarah thought would never happen. She was glad that she'd told Linda and Jade the truth because it had dissolved their barriers and she found it easier to talk.

'Where's that French yoga teacher? He gave me a rose last night and told me he lives in a huge Chateau. He also manages a vineyard for his elderly parents. We spoke for quite a while at the end of the evening.'

'Lucky you. I didn't see that,' said Jade.

'That's because you were out cold in your tent,' replied Linda, who was smiling at her.

'Andre,' he's gorgeous. I'm jealous,' said Jade, who suddenly realised they were talking about the handsome Frenchman.

'Jealous of me? Unfortunately, I'm married, and I can't have another affair.'

'You can't?' asked Jade.

'Can't, is a very negative word,' answered Sarah.

'We'll see,' replied Linda, looking at them both!

'That means, yes, because Linda doesn't know the word no, but we're working on it!' replied Jade laughing.

'Things are often work in progress! I'm giving up the stick I beat myself up with and learning to enjoy life. I need to say yes; more often,' answered Sarah.

'Sounds like a plan. Come on; you two, keep pedalling. We have to get the bikes back in fifteen minutes, and we still have one kilometre to go,' replied Linda, who just wanted to return her bike and look for Andre!

CHAPTER 16

GOING HOME

Cameron finally arrived at his parents' home late in the afternoon. His heart was heavy because he was disappointed that he'd left France so quickly before sorting things out with Sarah. He knew she was angry with him, but he had far more urgent matters on his mind.

'Cameron, thank goodness you're back,' said his mother.

'Yeah, I'm back. Hello, little one. How's my baby boy then?'

'He's not such a baby now you know, and he spent half the night screaming for his Mum! Violet is still in the hospital, and she's going to be there for another week. After that, she will need to rest. I hope you're willing to give up your free time?'

'Yes, of course, that's why I took the next available flight, as soon as I saw your message. But isn't having an appendix out a routine op, nowadays?'

'No, it wasn't Cameron, because it burst, and Violet nearly died. We've had endless trips to and from the hospital, and we're exhausted now.

'I'm glad you're back, Cameron. We knew you were dancing but looking after your son is far more important,' his father said.

Cameron was shocked. His father looked tired and drawn. Looking after Antonne must have taken its toll on them both. His parents retired a few years ago, but they still led busy lives with many interests.

'I thought he was staying here until Violet was better?' asked Cameron, who suddenly realised the impact caring for Antonne would have on his social life.

'We can look after him for a few days a week, but he's your son, and you need to take responsibility for him. We've agreed with Violet that we'll have him Monday to Friday and he can stay with you at the weekends, at least until she comes home,' his mother explained.

'Do I have a choice?' Cameron asked.

'No son, you don't,' his father said firmly.

When Owen put his foot down, that was it. Cameron knew it was futile to argue with him. He respected that, but he wondered how he'd cope with minimal experience looking after a toddler? Still, he would have to step up and learn. It couldn't be that difficult!

'I don't understand why you didn't contact me earlier? It happened last week, so why didn't you tell me then? I wouldn't have gone to France.' he said, suddenly realising the seriousness of the situation.

'We thought it was just a simple operation, or we would have been in touch. Violet's parents were going to look after him, but they got flu, so we stepped in. We didn't think you'd be able to get the time off work. We didn't realise you were dancing until we saw it on your social media!' his father continued.

'Well, I'm here now. Hey there buddy,' Cameron said lifting Antonne onto his hip. 'Shall we go into the garden to look for birds?'

'Take this bread', said Lucinda, he likes feeding the birds. He loves the outdoors. If you take him for walks, it keeps him interested. You can take some of his toys home. I'm sure the two of you will bond in a couple of days.'

'Thanks, Mum, I should have been here for my little buddy! How's Violet now? Is she feeling any better?'

'Like, I said, she's going to be at least another week in the hospital and then she will need to take it very easy when she comes home.'

'I'll go and see her in a couple of days, but I'll send a card. I can visit when you have Antonne and when she comes out, I'll look after them both.'

Cameron suddenly felt emotional, which was rare. He'd always expected Violet to cope with Antonne and he had never considered what would happen if she was ill. His son was a gorgeous child with big inquisitive sparkly eyes! Why hadn't he noticed that before? There was so much he could teach this little fella. His parents were right, he'd never bonded with him, but now he had the chance. What had he done all his life apart from thinking about himself? He had been so focused on his work, his meetings, earning money and dancing that he'd not given a second thought to her or his son, since they parted. Things had to change because this little guy needed him. They both might find it hard to adapt to the changes, but he would make it work somehow. He had to. What happened if Violet didn't get better? She had nearly died. He felt terrible.

'Daddy,' Antonne said and pulled at his shirt.

'Daddy, wow that's great, at least he remembers me,' said Cameron beaming.

'No, all men are Daddies,' replied his mother.

'Well, I need to change that. You don't have to worry, I understand what I have to do, and if you want to fetch Antonne's suitcase, I'll pack up his clothes and toys and take him with me tonight.'

'Cameron, you don't have to do that? Stay here tonight then you can have our help. You can take him home at the weekend. We'll have him when you go back to work.'

Cameron felt relieved. He wanted to bond with Antonne, but it would take time, and he didn't want him to scream his head off when they arrived at the flat. There wasn't much room at home because his spare room was full to the ceiling with speakers, musical instruments and old computers. He'd have to sleep this little fella in with him. That would be a new experience for them both. At least they had some bonding time before they were on their own.

A huge crow suddenly landed on the grass.

'Crow', shouted Antonne, as he started to jump up and down.

'Yes, crow,' replied Cameron, 'caw, caw',

'Apple,' replied Antonne, and he ran into the kitchen!

CHAPTER 17

PERFECT TIMING

The early evening sun gently shone on the group as they congregated around a small brick barbeque. They had bought some charcoal from the camping shop which required the minimum effort to burn, and after thirty minutes, the food was already sizzling. Andre took charge because he knew how to barbeque. He'd caught Linda's attention as she stood to the side of him, drinking a glass of white wine.

'Tell me a little more about the Chateau?' she asked.

'Well, it's about twenty kilometres from here. It's beautiful there, plus we have a huge vineyard.'

'You have a vineyard too? Do you make your wine on the premises?'

'Oui, c'est bon vin,' Andre replied with a look of pride on his face, 'and we do make the wine at the Chateau!'

'I love good wine. It's one of the good things in life. That steak looks rare, Andre! Can you cook it a bit longer, please?' asked Linda.

Andre laughed, 'that's how we eat our steak here.'

'Yuk,' said Jade. Meat makes me feel sick. I'm so glad I'm a vegetarian. I hope someone has put some veggie burgers on for me, or I'll starve!'

Sarah stood away from the others. There was still no text from Cameron. She wanted an apology about the earring which had belonged to Jade. It was probably a waste of time because he appeared too arrogant to make amends with anyone! She thought it incredible that he should pursue her so relentlessly when he had been sleeping with both Linda and Jade. What kind of man would do that? The realisation that he wasn't the person she thought, quickly crept over her, but she still felt upset. If she knew what he was like, why did she want any contact with him? It was madness. If only she'd told him to fuck off when he first entered the Yurt. But strangely, as soon as Cameron disappeared from the beach, the weekend lost its buzz. Was she disappointed because she'd thought he was someone he wasn't? That had happened before! It was odd that he disappeared so quickly.

Sarah picked up a clean fork and turned over some veggie burgers.

'Jade do you want one of these? If you do, make sure Andre doesn't touch them with that meaty tong thing, or we won't be able to eat them.'

'What meaty thong thing? I've been looking in the wrong direction,' replied Jade, who continued to laugh, while she poured yet, more wine!'

'Eat something, Jade, or you won't be able to dance later. You don't want to crash out in your tent, like last night or you will miss all the fun!'

'Ah, she's drinking the wine from the Chateau, that's strong', answered Andre, giving Linda a wink.

'Really' replied Linda, as she knocked back her glass. 'It's been a long day.'

'The night is young', Andre replied, in perfect English.

Linda marvelled at him. He was gorgeous. If only her French were half as good as his English but she knew how to communicate by touch. Cameron had taught her that. Her touch was the best in the world. She ran a single finger down

Andre's arm, and he smiled. She knew she was flirting, but it was fun, and she couldn't help herself.

'Your steak is ready, Madam,' he declared, looking into Linda's eyes.

'Merci, vous êtes le parfait gentleman.'

'And you are a perfect English Rose,' Andre replied, as he leaned forward to kiss Linda on the lips.

'I'm getting out of here,' announced Jade. 'You two make me feel like dancing!' As Jade started to walk away with her veggie burger, she suddenly noticed a text from Brian.

'Hi Jade, I hope you are having a great time? Please can you call me on WhatsApp?' Jade was surprised that Brian had WhatsApp? She could search for him, but she felt slightly unsettled because he was in the mental box that she'd allocated for work. Jade knew Brian respected her opinion, but it wasn't a good time. She would call him later when she was by herself. She didn't want to risk saying the wrong thing when she'd been drinking!

It was still a beautiful warm evening, and the others had started to dance. Jade was unsure if she was capable of dancing, so she took her shoes off and tiptoed through the long grass to her tent. She vowed not to lie down, or she might crash out like last night and miss a good evening. Brian had now appeared on her WhatsApp, so Jade decided to call. At least it would get it out of the way, and she could enjoy the rest of the evening without worrying.

The phone rang at the other end of the line, and Brian took his time to answer. There was a lot of noise in the background, and she wondered if he was in a bar.

'Hi, Brian, what's up?'

'Oh Jade, I'm under a load of stress here. That woman Michele keeps texting me to ask if we can meet again. I thought she had got the message, but she hasn't. It's over. Now I'm worried she might turn up on my doorstep.'

'Well she's here in France, so she isn't going anywhere! Please, don't worry. I will keep an eye on her. I can try and distract her by steering her towards a good-looking Frenchman! It shouldn't be too difficult for her to find someone with dresses halfway up her arse.' Jade continued.

'Halfway up her arse! Jade, you have a great way of putting things but thinking about it, she always wore very short dresses even to our business meetings.'

Jade wanted to ask him if that's what he'd liked about her, but she thought better of it, especially after the wine!

'I think my marriage is over; things have fallen apart. I'll tell you about it when you get back. I wondered if Michele was in France. Why would she text me when she's with you? Isn't she having fun?'

'I'm sure she is. I guess she doesn't want to let go,' replied Jade, who realised she was becoming too involved!

'Well, cheers, Jade. You're a diamond. I don't know where I'd be without you. Can you please try and keep this between us because I've already wrecked my home life, so I don't want to be the new talk of the office!'

'Brian, everything you say to me is confidential. I don't play Chinese whispers.'

'Good, I'm glad to hear it. Thanks for letting me bend your ear. I'll see you next week.'

'Ok, bye for now,' answered Jade, who didn't want to talk about next week when she was on holiday trying to have fun!

Jade quickly grabbed a pair of red sparkly dance shoes and headed to the marquee. Her heels were nearly three inches tall, but she still managed to dance in them. As soon as she arrived, she noticed there were more French men tonight, and she looked forward to the variety of dance moves. It was going to be a good night. Her first dance of the evening with a gorgeous French man, in his mid-thirties. As they danced, her mind drifted back to Brian and Michele. Did she have the courage to tell her to back off, or was it none of her business? If Michele continued to upset Brian, she might lose it with her? The woman must have a screw loose to keep texting him while she was here in this stunningly beautiful place when he'd already told her it was over.

Jade knew that if she drank much more, she would likely put her foot in it because she usually did! It felt as if Brian was the underdog, and she wanted to protect him, but why? If Michele was a minx, was it her problem? Then again, Brian had made it her issue by telephoning her. Why did this have to happen? She was always picking up the pieces.

Michele was standing by the bar in a short sparkly dress. She looked gorgeous and had an air of sophistication, and for a minute, Jade felt envious. These career women seldom carried any extra pounds and looked stunning in whatever they wore. Men ate out of their hands, but they rarely committed. It was a wicked game.

Jade walked towards the bar and stood about six foot away to observe her. The two French guys with her appeared utterly enthralled and were speaking to her in broken English. Jade heard one of them say he needed a new accountant and was asking for her number.

As the men moved towards the dance floor Michele turned to Jade and said 'Hi, did you have fun at the beach today, I saw you swimming?'

'Yeah, it was good, but Cameron went home, so we've lost one of our best dancers. I'm not sure why he left, some sort of emergency,' she replied.

'Cameron, is he the gorgeous black guy I danced with last night? Has he gone? I can't believe that. Where does he dance?'

Jade felt annoyed at Michele's interest in Cameron and took a long deep breath.

'I've had a text from Brian today. He said that you wouldn't leave him alone. It's over Michele. He isn't interested in you.'

Michele looked at Jade for a few moments in silence, then started to speak in a sarcastic tone. 'I don't know why you are so keen to protect him. Maybe you have a thing about him? Not that Brian would ever look at you, being his receptionist. No one takes you seriously Jade, not even at salsa!'

Jade felt her heart beating very fast and started to feel sick. She couldn't decide whether to walk away or reply to this woman who was proving to be a bitch. She was suddenly aware she was standing there open-mouthed and needed to get herself together. Fortunately, Linda appeared, followed by Andre.

'Are you alright, you look a bit shaken?' asked Linda.

'I'm stirred and shaken Linda. Please, can you fetch me another drink because I need one? No, not the Bacardi, some of that special Vineyard White if there's any left? I've just learned an important lesson, not to interfere in a situation that has nothing to do with you because it leaves egg on your face!'

'You've had un oeuf? Sorry, I don't understand. Would you like to visit the vineyard with Linda tomorrow?' asked Andre, who looked confused.

'Yes, that will be great because I have had un oeuf!' Jade replied, forcing a smile, but she still felt shaken. No one took her seriously. Well, she would soon see about that!

'Fantastic, we'll make an early start. It's an enormous place, and I want to see as much of it as possible. Have you got any flat shoes, Jade?' asked Linda.

CHAPTER 18

LOOK ON THE HORIZON

The early morning mist hovered over the vines as Linda and Jade looked in wonder at the neat green rows which stretched as far as their eyes could see.

'They won't be ready to pick until the beginning of September, so we have quite a few weeks to go, but you can already see that this year is going to be good.'

'Do you have bad years then?' asked Jade.

'Yes, we've had bad years. Last year wasn't very good because it rained a lot, which was rare. It depends on the amount of sun.'

'Who picks all these vines? It must be a massive job,' Linda asked.

'We have regulars who come every year. I keep a list, but most of them are locals that live in the surrounding villages. The picks can go on for several weeks, depending on the size of the crop,' answered Andre.

Linda once again marvelled at Andre's grasp of the English language, if only she could speak French half as well.

'Where is the Chateau then, we didn't pass it on the way?' she asked.

'You can't see it from the road because of the trees, but it's over there, in the distance.'

'Where?' repeated Linda, 'I still can't see it.'

'Look on the horizon,' Andre said as he gently put his arm around Linda to point her in the right direction.

'I can see it on my own,' said Jade, who felt slightly embarrassed by their intimacy. 'It looks like a castle in a storybook.'

'Oh, it has a story,' replied Andre, it's been in my family for many years, and I work hard managing it for my parents. I also hold Yoga Retreats there in the summer.'

'Do you? Yoga Retreats, what do your parents think of that?' asked Linda.

'So long as the grapes are picked, they don't mind,' replied Andre.

'Do you have any red?' asked Jade.

'Rouge,' Oui c'est tres bonne.'

'He means it's good,' Linda explained to Jade.

'I know what he means. I know the important things, Linda!'

'Ok, let's continue to walk, and I can show you the rest of the vines, then we can have a coffee in the restaurant. We don't grow much red so it won't take long,' Andre explained, hoping the girls would stop bickering and keep up the pace.

'You have a restaurant?' asked Linda, who was now feeling overwhelmed by such an interesting man!

'Yes, we have a restaurant, and I'm looking for staff. We need a new manager for the rest of the summer because the lady who runs it wants to move nearer her family. People love working here and stay for years.'

'Oh, that's the perfect job for you then Jade if you want to learn something new? You would enjoy the wine as well,' replied Linda giving her a nudge.

'Actually,' I am looking for a mature woman, one with plenty of life experience so that she can understand our guests' needs,' replied Andre looking directly at Linda.

Linda went quiet for a minute and looked at Jade. A new job in France, the thought terrified her, but at the same time, it could be a new way forward.

'So where would this mature woman live?' she asked tentatively.

'In the chateau, of course. We have many rooms. The place is empty half the year, and it needs someone to bring it to life.'

'Shall we go for coffee, and you can tell me more about it?' asked Linda, who was feeling exhilarated.

Jade was bored. Linda was stealing the show, which was no surprise. Even if she were interested in the role, it would be a waste of time applying because Linda already had her name on it! She wondered if Andre had invented the position to draw her in, but he sounded genuine when he said they had been looking for the right person for several months.

They walked through some glass doors into a small barn filled with white wooden tables and chairs. Jade had never seen such a gorgeous space. The restaurant had been beautifully decorated with dried flowers, rustic ornaments and tasteful pictures and had a very relaxing atmosphere.

'Wow, this is incredible,' Jade remarked as she stared at the heavily beamed ceiling.

'Everyone loves it here. If we find a little space, you ladies must teach me how to improve my salsa because I have what you English say, two left feet.'

'No, you don't. You are a natural dancer with a good lead,' Linda answered warmly.

'I find you sexy,' replied Jade.

Andre laughed then said, 'if you are interested in the job, Linda, let me know soon because I'll only be around for a few more days. Then I have to work.'

'You call that vineyard work?' said Jade laughing.

'Jade if you are going to keep being rude, you'll have to sit on another table,' Linda snapped.

'Sorry,' she said 'I'm under stress.'

Jade flicked through her phone and noticed that she had two missed calls from Brian and a text message.

'I've left Jade. Please call me when you get back home. If you see Michele, please don't say anything to her because she has a nasty tongue. You'd be better to keep away from her if you can.'

Now he tells me, thought Jade! Michele had magnified all her feelings of low self-esteem, and she had just taken it on the chin. It would be impossible to keep away from her the whole weekend. It was a pity that Brian became involved with her in the first place! She felt sorry for him but was it more than that, was Michele, right? Did she have feelings for him? They had always got on well, but he was her boss. One minute she was having sex with Cameron hoping that it would turn into a relationship and now she was thinking about Brian. What was going on?

'Ok, Jade, let's go. Andre is going to drive us around the edge of his estate then drive us back.'

As they walked back to the car park, Jade noticed that Andre and Linda were walking very close to each other. Their body language said it all. It would be a surprise if Linda took the job though because she'd have to give up her home, husband and poor Peanut! She was too fond of that dog to leave him behind, but Linda was full of surprises. Who would have thought she would have had an affair with Cameron and for so long! Where was her soulmate now? He'd done a runner. Perhaps Cameron had other dark secrets that he kept to himself!

CHAPTER 19

PLAYER NO MORE

VIOLET

Violet felt tired and unwell, but she had accepted the hospital was the best place to recover. She was relieved that her parents were over the flu and would soon be able to visit. She missed Antonne and was worried about him. Was Cameron capable of looking after a two-year-old? If not, he'd just have to learn because she was too sick to look after him. Violet wished they were still a family. They had argued while they were together, but it was easier than living on her own. It was tough having to work in the restaurant with a young child when she had to continually take Antonne to her parents or ask friends to look after him. She earned so little. At least when they were together, they made enough to live on, and they could go out.

The nurse removed Violet's oxygen mask. Her levels were up so she could lay and relax. The doctor told her she should be out at the weekend, but Violet found it hard to imagine when she struggled to walk to the toilet, twenty feet away.

Violet looked around her. She had received many presents and cards. There was one from Cameron, which said, 'Hi Violet, I will visit you soon and look after you both when you come home.' She wasn't sure what Cameron meant by that. Although Violet wanted him to come home, she had convinced herself he never would. Cameron didn't like commitment, and he'd declared himself a free spirit, unless having the experience of looking after Antonne, had changed him? Was it possible to have a late wake-up call? Her friends and work colleagues had visited several times, but Cameron hadn't appeared! One of her friends had even offered to look after her and Antonne until she regained her strength. She sighed; going home could be hard work, when she was unable to lift, so it made sense to accept her friend's offer, but Cameron had texted to say he would pick them up. It sounded like he planned to move back in for a few weeks.

Violet drifted in, and out of sleep which the nurse explained was a good thing, but she was also beginning to feel restless. She just wanted to be back home in her comfortable little house. The house that Cameron had walked out of a few years ago when they had only just finished the decorating! Violet had never understood why he left when they had worked so hard, but Cameron was always chasing some project, woman or illusion that kept him away from her. She was happy Antonne loved his grandparents. They were fantastic people, and perhaps in time, Cameron would be like them and take more responsibility.

On the other hand, she could recover from this and meet someone new, a good father for Antonne. His parents explained that he'd been away in France. She wondered what he was doing there, salsa? She'd heard that Cameron liked to dance and was good at it. He was good at most things. He was intelligent, good looking and fabulous at conversation, which made her feel inadequate. It wasn't completely his fault, she realised that now. If only she had taken her Science Degree as her parents suggested a few years ago because right now her only option was working in the restaurant. It was impossible to focus on her career when she had to earn money and look after her son.

Violet stretched her arm out to the cabinet to re-read Cameron's card.

'Be careful, young lady. You know you shouldn't be doing that. Let me get it for you,' said the nurse in a loud voice.

'Ah thanks, sorry,' she replied.

'It must be from someone special if you're stretching that far for it?' the nurse continued.

'Yeah, it's from my ex. Cameron. He's looking after my little boy, and he's going to look after us both when I leave,' replied Violet.

'You know something. I heard this salsa song the other day called 'You,' or something like that, it made me want to dance. I guess the guy suddenly woke up and realised he hadn't appreciated his woman. It's on YouTube. I hope your man wakes up too!'

'Yeah, some guys just keep looking. I'm not sure what they are looking for, but no one can run from themselves forever.'

'YOU, need to think about YOU, for a while, by the looks of it.'

'What's the name of that song again so that I can listen to it on my phone.'

'YOU', she repeated a little loudly and suddenly took a salsa step!'

Violet smiled, then opened the card and looked at Cameron's handwriting. The same familiar feelings came flooding back, and she realised that despite everything, she still loved him. Violet closed the card and laid it down on the bed. As she drifted into a peaceful sleep, her head was repeating, he'll be here soon but her body needed to recover, and she could no longer fight it!

CHAPTER 20

BACK TO THE GRIND

Jade was back at work. The excitement of the salsa weekender was over, and she'd had a fantastic time in France, enjoying some of the best dancing in her life. Jade had loved dancing with the French guys and had added some of their numbers to her mobile. She had also found a few of them on Facebook, so they could start connecting.

Brian seemed decidedly moody since her return to work. She realised he was struggling and had decided not to interfere unless asked because he needed to sort his life out! Thankfully Michele had stopped hassling him because she'd met someone new at another dance class. Brian was relieved that the woman had finally moved on. He'd explained to Jade that he had left the marital home and was now renting a flat next to the Marina, which had surprised everyone in the office! Jade never gossiped about Brian, but despite this, most of the office knew his situation.

Jade received a phone call from Linda today, asking if she would like to meet for a quick drink. She explained that she was going to take the job at the Vineyard, but Jade still didn't want to take her seriously. How could Linda leave her husband and children? It was unimaginable. But Linda often had that element of surprise, which had caught her out on many occasions! Hopefully, she'd stay because Linda was a good mate, even if they had shared the same man. Things had become a lot easier since Linda had met her new soulmate, and she no longer talked about Cameron. He was now history!

Sarah was a different kettle of fish. She was still very private and didn't want to share the intimate details of her life, but Jade noticed the three of them had bonded since their return from France. Sarah was a lot more friendly. But she would never be entirely one of the girls because her spiritual interests kept her pretty busy. Jade was intrigued. She had learned some great things by listening to Sarah. She had taught her about detachment, and she felt a lot better since practising that. Being constantly empathic wasn't necessary. Jade didn't know there was such a thing as an empath until Sarah explained there were many people like her, but it was now time to think of herself!

'Jade just focus on you for a while and step back because you will honestly feel better. Take back your power. If people want your help, they will ask you, but don't be everyone's agony aunt. If you do it too often, you will soak up everyone's negative emotions, and feel exhausted.'

'Ah right, maybe I need to read up about this. It sounds toxic,' Jade replied.

When it came to knowledge, Sarah was the person to be around. She had even tried her yoga class last week, and balanced on one leg! It had to happen eventually! The heron position or something like that! She was on her way to becoming a 'leggy bird,' which was something she had always wanted! Jade knew her confidence had grown since her return from France mainly because she had kept away from men. Casual sex had never been fun because she was too sensitive. Destructive behaviours were part of her past, which enabled her to stay in a positive zone!

When Jade was alone, she often thought about Brian. She realised that any forward movement between them would have to come from him. He had finished with Michele, but he was still in pain from his marriage and had baggage to work through. He had recently asked her about salsa. Where was it held, and what time were the classes? She was a little surprised by this and suggested that he joined the beginner's group, which started in two weeks. He still appeared to be tired and stressed some of the time, so maybe dancing would help, but Jade had kept her promise to herself not to be empathic or suggest anything unless he reached out. At last, she was having fun, so why take on Brian's headache?

As soon as Linda returned from France, her only thought was, had Adrian walked Peanut? She immediately noticed that the gap between them had widened. He was curious about the weekend which irritated Linda because she didn't want to talk about it. He had even started to dance a few salsa steps by following a YouTube, which drove her crazy.

'You show me then,' Adrian asked. 'Why do you have all the fun, while I'm left holding the baby?' he said, looking towards their dog.

'That's because you're always working, and you don't make time for fun,' replied Linda. 'I've got used to having fun on my own now because you forced me into it and now you don't like it. That's ironic.'

'Well, it's never too late to change?' muttered Adrian.

'But it is too late,' Linda replied, sounding sad. 'You've thought about your career your whole life, and now I want to do something, so things are going to change.'

'Change how?' asked Adrian, who looked utterly baffled by her statement.

'If you want to get a job, Linda, please get one. The kids left home years ago, and there has been nothing to stop you furthering your career.'

'What career?'

'Your career as a florist,' said Adrian. He had no idea where this was going, but he'd started to raise his voice!

'No, I don't want to be a florist. I'm moving to the South of France to manage a restaurant.'

'Don't be stupid, Linda, you couldn't manage a restaurant, you have no experience. I don't mean to be cruel, but this has to be a joke?'

'No, it's not a fucking joke Adrian, I met someone when I was in France, and he's offered me a job.'

'Oh, so you've got a new lover? What happened to the other one, the black guy, was he bored?'

Linda fell silent.

'So, you thought I didn't know about Cameron? You must think I'm stupid!'

'I know who he is Linda and where he lives. Did you imagine no one would tell me?'

'Why didn't you say something, then?' she asked.

'Because you are Linda and unbelievably, I love you. I don't want to lose you even if our sex life is history.'

Linda looked at Adrian and didn't know what to say. Here stood the man she'd been married to for thirty years, and she knew that she didn't love him, not in the way that he wanted her to.

'I'm ...'

'No, don't say it. You must never be sorry for not loving someone. I guess I've known for ages and I couldn't accept it. Do you have to go to France? It seems a little drastic, bit of a whim?'

'Yes, I'm going because I need to. I must see if I can manage on my own. If I can survive as an independent woman, have a career and build a new life where I choose.'

'So, you haven't chosen any of this. This house, this neighbourhood and your life with Peanut and me. What will happen to him?'

'I don't know,' replied Linda 'but I know I can't stay.'

'Salsa went to your brain! You were alright before you started that!'

'I was alright?'

'Yeah you were content, then the sex dropped off because of your multiple affairs!'

'I haven't had multiple affairs, Adrian!'

'So that makes it better, does it? I hope he was worth it? Oh, just go Linda, but you'll have to leave Peanut. You can also tell the kids because they'll be heartbroken.'

Tears streamed down Linda's face. She knew Adrian had gone into the garden to stomp around his vegetable patch. He always did that when he couldn't handle situations. But today was different. She wouldn't be surprised if he started hurling his vegetables! For the first time, she wondered if she was doing the right thing. She knew it would be hard to tell him, but she hadn't expected this. Her heartfelt wrenched from her body, but she didn't know why because she had been sure going to France was the right thing. Now everything suddenly felt different. What if it didn't work out and she had to come back? There was no way that Adrian would allow her back because he was so damn stubborn. Linda decided to go up to her room to get away from him for a while. She wanted to call Andre to make sure he still wanted her to come. If he wasn't serious, then all this drama was a complete waste of time!

'Yes, Linda, I'm waiting for you. Pack your suitcase and come next week because we need you. The other lady's left.' explained Andre.

Linda suddenly felt shocked that her daydream had turned into reality. She grabbed her suitcase from the top of her wardrobe and hastily started to pack. It would be easier to call the children in the morning because it wasn't the right time. Adrian would hear it all over again. Their children were both adults with relationships of their own, so she hoped they would understand. Surely, they realised she was unhappy?

As Linda packed her clothes, her mind was on Peanut, who had been her companion for so many years. How could she leave him? When she had settled into her new home, she'd come back for him. Adrian wouldn't be able to look after him with all his work commitments. Part of her felt, what have I done, and the other part of her was relieved. She'd get a flight tomorrow after she'd told the children. That meant it would be her last night in this house with Adrian, so she'd make an effort to be civil to him even if he thought she was a slut! Multiple affairs, where had he heard that! There had only been

Cameron, and despite Andre, she knew he would be the one that remained in her heart. She wasn't sure what the arrangements were, but Andre had said there was a room ready in the Chateau, there were wages, and she had the use of a car, complete independence! No doubt it would be arduous work with hours of standing on her feet, but she was still young and fit and was looking forward to the challenge!

Linda walked downstairs to stroke Peanut. Her heart would break, saying goodbye to him tomorrow. She found him curled in his basket, looking very still. She was in floods of tears at the thought of leaving him behind. 'I'll come and get you soon, don't you worry,' she said, as she moved closer to him. Then she noticed that he wasn't breathing and suddenly realised he was dead.

CHAPTER 21

THURSDAY - SALSA NIGHT

It was Thursday evening, and Jade was looking forward to dancing at the salsa club. She wondered whether Cameron would be there. It was now a few months since they'd returned from France. She had been too busy to dance much since she'd started attending a gym, but every cell in her body missed the sound of those Cuban rhythms, and she needed to dance. There had been a horrible empty feeling in her heart since Linda left. She couldn't believe how quickly it happened. Her friend just packed up and left. When they met for a quick goodbye drink, Linda couldn't stop crying over Peanut. She seemed to be more upset about leaving the dog than parting from Adrian, then Peanut died! Linda also said her children took the news badly and weren't speaking to her. Things were complicated when she first arrived, but Andre was lovely, and it was a great new start. Jade thought Linda was a brilliant friend. Even if she had sometimes appeared a little selfish, her leaving had hit her hard. Linda messaged to say that Jade could stay at the Chateau for a few days while the parents were in Italy so Jade was excited about the prospect of returning to France for a short holiday if she could fit it in!

The guest suite at the Chateau Blanche had an elegant bedroom, an adjoining bathroom and lounge, which Linda considered extremely spacious. She'd written a long email to Jade last night to explain that she was now making headway with the job and Andre was pleased. Jade was relieved because it had initially sounded a bit of a nightmare. She hadn't known where she was sleeping because Andre hadn't discussed it with his parents, or told them she was the new manager! The previous manager had lived in her property a few kilometres away, so they weren't expecting to provide rooms for the new one. There had been several long arguments between Andre and his parents which Linda had unfortunately witnessed! She was grateful to have a limited understanding of their language, or their arguing would have upset her!

Jade smiled. She knew Linda could do it because she was determined and reliable. Andre was a nice guy who needed an organiser around him, and Linda fitted the bill! Jade decided to email her back tomorrow. If anything exciting happened tonight, she could add it to the email because she always enjoyed any news about salsa!

As Jade walked into Club Cubanica, she felt the stir of both excitement and nerves at seeing the others. The first person she encountered was George sitting in the bar.

'Hello Jade, what's happened to your friend?' he asked.

'Which friend? I have quite a few? Do you mean, Sarah, Linda or Harriett?

'The slim, attractive one. The good dancer who was with us in France.'

'Ah, you mean Linda? She's gone to work in a Chateau in the South of France, not far from the campsite. Andre offered her a job running his restaurant,' replied Jade.

'Really, you are bloody kidding! She comes back from a weekender, then leaves her marriage to live in France, just like that?'

'Yeah, said Jade, 'it's called confronting a problem head-on, or grabbing life while you can, whatever resonates.'

'Good God. Yes, I know what you mean. Since I came back from France, I've stopped wearing a shirt and tie, not even to work. My wife says I look better in a tee-shirt. All this dancing has made me lose my belly. Grab life while you can, yeah, I like that!'

'But are you going to do it? Don't go overboard and lose the tee-shirt because we saw enough of that in France!' Jade said jokingly. I hope your wife is doing your washing now? Excuse me George, but I've just seen a familiar face. I have to go and dance.'

George smiled and put down his beer. Jade was hot, but he'd always fancied Linda. Just his luck that she'd found a good-looking Frenchman! Had he got something he hadn't? George watched Jade walk over to a tall blonde man standing at the edge of the dance floor. They appeared to know each other, which he found intriguing.

'So, you're here at last?' said Jade. As she smiled at Brian, she felt a wave of giggly girlishness surface.

'Yep, I'm here, what next?' asked Brian, who was already looking relaxed and well-adjusted to his new surroundings.

'Well, you've missed the beginners, so I guess you're in the intermediates with me once the social dancing's finished,' replied Jade.

'Jade, I have a confession. I had some crossbody lessons with Michele, so I think I could manage this class, even if it is a different style. I can dance on time. Would you like to dance?'

Jade said nothing. She just took Brian's hand, which felt warm and friendly as he led her onto the dance floor. A slow salsa was playing, and she managed to follow his lead, despite dancing a different style.

'You're good,' she whispered as he turned her into a sombrero, 'and that's Cuban!'

'Yeah, I also had a few Cuban lessons on my own after Michele left. I think it's more my thing, so I've come here to learn a little more.'

'Yes, it is,' answered Jade grinning.

'How do you know what's my thing?'

'I don't really. I can't hear you very well,' Jade replied, laughing.

As she looked at Brian, she suddenly caught a slight twinkle in his eye that she'd never seen before. The serious and sometimes grey-faced man had miraculously turned into a dancing diva, and she wanted to laugh. Brian was no longer the serious man at the office. He had become just Brian, and she realised that despite her resistance, she felt an attraction.

When they'd finished the dance, Brian asked her if she'd like a drink. 'Yes, please, that would be great,' she replied, 'lime and soda!'

'Go and dance with your friends Jade. I'm sure you have plenty of them. I'll see you in the line-up.'

Ten minutes later, after Brian had lined up with the others to dance, Jade realised he didn't look out of place. He was discussing the benefits of dancing cross body and Cuban together with George, which meant he could dance with more partners! Trust Brian to work that one out she thought. It was just like him. He's probably been studying a manual, but either way, he was good at it!

Sarah arrived and appeared remarkably happy.

'Hi Sarah, I haven't seen you for weeks. Are you ok?' Jade whispered.

'Yeah, I'm okay. I'm looking forward to dancing as it's been all yoga for the last few weeks.

'Where's Linda?'

'Linda, well, that is a long story. Maybe we should catch up over a drink?' replied Jade.

'Where's Cameron then?' I thought he'd have turned up by now, even if he made himself unpopular. It's been weeks.' Sarah asked, looking a little shocked.

'He messaged to say that he isn't coming to salsa because he's looking after his son for a few weeks,' replied Jade.

'His son, I didn't know he had one, did you?'

'No, I didn't. I know fuck all about Cameron!'

'Well, that's two of us then! Who is that good-looking blonde guy at the front of the line-up? By the way, they've started, so we better stop chatting and join in?'

'That's Brian, my boss'.

'Your boss, you've got to be kidding, I'd like to be bossed by him.'

'He's taken! You, need to get in line, Sarah. There are loads of things I want to tell you so let's talk soon over a drink or soda!'

Sarah smiled. She couldn't believe Cameron had a child. Did that mean he was married? Why was she still thinking about him? After all, he hadn't bothered to keep in touch, but he had been texting Jade? Perhaps he'd make contact when he was through looking after his son? But were you ever through looking after your child? Sarah noticed Jade smiling at Brian, who was returning the interest. That's what love looks like, Sarah thought, as she looked on with envy. Even if I haven't got it right now, I'm sure it will come soon because I've started to love myself!

Brian enjoyed the salsa class and dancing with Jade. It felt as if he'd been wading through treacle for weeks, but this had begun to clear. Brian had made a new resolution to have fixed days for socialising; otherwise, his life would turn into a never-ending work schedule. He had noticed his feelings for Jade a few months ago, but the situation was confusing. He didn't even know why he had chased Michele when Jade was the woman he wanted. She had something loving and earthy about her. A kind of innocence he seldom saw in people. The young lady was also very good at her job and was an asset to his company. He had wrestled with the prospect of becoming involved with her, in case working together became awkward, so when Michele appeared, she was a good distraction, but it didn't stop the passion he felt for Jade.

Brian was happy to be living on his own. It had been hell, leaving his family home and children, but he was already experiencing the benefits. It was easier to relax, and the locality enabled him to socialise. He'd seen Jade out with her friends a few times, and despite being on his own, he decided not to join them in case it was imposing. Tonight, was different; it was the perfect opportunity for them to see each other in a new way. He was now a different man. He felt free, but he was still looking for a companion, not just sex, as it had been with Michele. Thank God, she'd gone. It had got to the point where he had to be nasty to get rid of her. What was wrong with her? He'd explained from the off what it was about, and she had been happy with that until she became hooked!

Brian opened the door to his flat and walked into his lounge. It was tiny in comparison to his former home but did that matter? It was all brand new and convenient. He was slowly adjusting but wished he could cosy up with someone to watch a movie! He decided to take out his mobile and call Jade. He knew it was a little spontaneous because it was late, but he couldn't help himself. He just wanted to reach out to her.'

'Hi, Jade,'

'Hi,' Jade replied. She knew it was Brian.

'What are you doing?' he asked.

'What do you mean, what am I doing? I'm in bed because I've got work tomorrow, remember?'

'Ah, yes. I just phoned to say how much I enjoyed the class tonight. I love Rueda.'

'Yeah, it's great. Are you coming next week then?'

'I think so, as long as you are ok about it?'

'Of course, why wouldn't I be? Anyway, it isn't my class. I enjoyed dancing with you tonight. It was fun.'

'Great, I enjoyed it too. I was wondering if you'd like to go out to dinner tomorrow evening?'

'What, you mean a date?'

'Yes, a date.'

'That would be great! Let's go for it. Why not the world's our oyster.'

'We're just going on a date!'

'Cool, come and get me.'

'Ok, I will,' Brian said and was gone.

Later Jade discovered she had a feeling which she'd never experienced before. She was right; the world was her oyster, and this was the start of her journey.

CHAPTER 22

CAMERON AND VIOLET

Violet was pleased to discover that Cameron chose to move in with them until she was better and he'd now been with them for a couple of weeks. She'd noticed Antonne's behaviour had dramatically improved and there had been less of the terrible twos. Cameron had also cooked, although they'd eaten a lot of takeaways! He did well at cooking because he usually ate on the move, and Violet knew that he had never used a recipe book. Despite an improved friendship, Violet noticed their romantic relationship hadn't progressed. Cameron kept his distance, but he appeared to be happy enough in the carer role. She knew better than to dig for answers, knowing that Cameron could easily do a runner if she applied pressure. So, when he initially asked to sleep on the sofa, she found it easier to accept it.

Cameron didn't want to return to a relationship with Violet. He'd been there and done that, and it had never worked. But since

Antonne had become an important pa_
life, he knew he wanted to support them by
a friend to Violet. His mother and father \
pleased they were living together and had start_ _
to assume that their relationship would return to
the way it had been. Cameron firmly pointed out
to his parents that he couldn't commit to Violet
in the way she wanted. He wanted her to find
someone who could give her what she wanted
when her health returned! Violet hated Cameron
for saying this. She hoped that Cameron would
change his mind. But over the past few days, he
had become restless in the house, particularly in
the evenings. Cameron was continually checking
his phone and going out in the garden to have
private conversations. Violet asked if he missed
Salsa. Cameron said yes, of course, I do. I'm going
to return to classes soon. I'm not leaving here yet,
so don't panic, but I must stay in touch with my
dance friends. Violet had explained on numerous
occasions that she didn't want to stop him from
being a free spirit, but things had changed when
Antonne was born. If he needed to go out more
now, he should go because she understood the
need for freedom. If he needed to go out more,
he should go because she understood the need
for freedom.

Cameron grabbed a little space when he
went shopping. He'd texted Jade a few times to
tell her he wanted to return to dancing, but for
the last week or so, he'd been looking after his

child. Jade took ages to reply to his messages, which was odd. Even after France, Cameron felt they would remain friends. When he'd asked her about Linda, he couldn't believe what she told him. How the hell did that happen? He had a special bond with Linda. She had called them soul mates. He hadn't agreed, but sexually they were perfect for each other. He belonged in her body. Now Linda had fucked off with some French guy with an enormous Chateau. It affected his manhood!

'What's up,' asked Violet, seeing the look on Cameron's face when he'd returned from one of his little shopping trips!

'Oh, it's just a friend of mine, she's gone to live in France. She left her husband, the dog, everything, to live in France. No, the dog died!'

'Did you like her?'

'She was old, but I liked her, and I can't believe she left that quickly.'

'Well life changes and people move on, that's what they do,' answered Violet, who was now hastily dusting, while Antonne was having his nap.' I reckon her old man came to his senses and chucked her out.'

Cameron stood up and walked into the garden. He knew if he talked to Violet about anything, she'd get on his nerves. Sarah had been on his mind since they had got together in the Yurt. He knew she was angry about the earring, but if he apologised to her, perhaps she'd give him another chance. He was stupid to put it in his pocket, but when he looked in the mirror, he saw it embedded in his dreads!

Sarah was gorgeous, sexy and fun, but this energy stuff had taken her over. He wasn't sure if he could be the man she wanted. Even if he looked at that tantric book, he had too many dark corners. 'There had to be a connection?' Perhaps if he had taken the time to read it to the end, he would have understood it! He wasn't sure if he'd deleted it now with a load of other apps but if he wanted Sarah, he had to try harder! Perhaps it was time to make a call? Cameron was restless and wanted to spend time with someone other than Violet because she had started to drive him mad.

Cameron's phone rang for ages before Sarah answered. He was just about to finish the call when he heard a quiet voice say, 'Hello.'

'Sarah, how are you?'

'I'm okay, Cameron, thanks. I've been doing a lot of yoga and dancing. I'm back at the classes now. It's a bit quiet because some people have left.

'Yeah, I heard about Linda. I hope she enjoys her new life. It must be great to start again at her age,' Cameron replied, trying to sound cheerful and optimistic.

'Linda isn't old Cameron. Anyway, how are you?'

'I'm well. I've been busy being a Dad for a while, looking after my son. I thought it was about time we got to know each other properly, and his Mum needed me because she was in the hospital. She was extremely ill.'

'I'm very sorry to hear that, is that why you rushed home from France, just as the fun started?'

'Yeah, I had to look after the poor little sod, he must have wondered what on earth was going on.'

'So, you're back at your flat, now?'

'Yeah, of course, where did you think I was? Violet, Antonne's mum and I are just friends. I pop up to the house now and again to babysit, but she knows where we're at.'

'Really,' replied Sarah.

'So, did you enjoy our session in France?'

'Dance session, what do you mean by that? Or do you mean when you joined in the morning yoga class?'

'No, I meant when I took you on the floor of the Yurt?'

'Oh, that was a session, was it?'

'Well, what would you call it Sarah?'

'I would say I fucked you because I wanted you, then I found out that you've had 'sessions' with all of my friends!'

'Not all of them Sarah!'

'Are you sure about that?'

Why are you like this? You know you want me and I want you, so why don't we meet and get on with it?'

'Because I don't want to.'

'Ah, right! What do you want, Sarah?'

Cameron, I don't know why we are having this conversation. Jade told me you were living with Violet, and you can't even be honest about that. I don't want anything from you. If I see you dancing, fine, but I don't want you coming to yoga. We have nothing in common.

'Tantra?' replied Cameron wistfully.

'You don't know anything about tantra Cameron. It takes more than reading an eBook to understand it. I need to get on now because I'm teaching soon, so see you around.'

Cameron sighed. He was wasting his time with these salsa women. It would be better to find a woman who was into something different like golf or horse riding, anything but dancing. Jade was dating a guy from work, who was a great dancer and from what she said he was also good at everything else. She had also lost tons of weight by going to the gym. Part of him couldn't wait to see her, but perhaps he ought to just stay away before he got into more trouble! Linda was gone, and he didn't want to think about that, and Sarah had made it clear that he was wasting his time because he had used the word session! How would she have described it then? God, women were hard work!

As Cameron walked back into the house towards the lounge, he suddenly noticed the sound of laughter. Violet was teaching Antonne animal noises. Cameron suddenly felt a warmth towards her that he hadn't experienced for years! Violet was alright just a little annoying, but at least she didn't pretend to be someone she wasn't. Cameron had always felt a bit of a bastard walking out when Antonne was born, but he wanted to experience different women! Would it be so bad to stay with this woman, a wonderful mother who cared for his child? He wanted to be that person, but he still wasn't sure if it was possible. Violet was too good for him. Perhaps one day he could do it!

'Do you want to go to the park?' he asked. Antonne stood up and started jumping up and down, 'park, park, ducks, ducks,' until he had no more breath!

'Are you coming, Violet?'

'What you want me to come?'

'Yeah why not, you can hold the bread,' he said laughing.

'I have bread in bags ready. I always save the crusts for the ducks.'

'But are you up to the walk?' asked Cameron

'Yes, if I can hold your arm because I haven't got all my strength back yet.'

'Yeah sure,' he said.

The park was busy when they arrived there, fifteen minutes later. Cameron took his son out of the buggy and lifted him onto his hip.

'Show me the ducks then because I can't see any,' he said, looking in the pond.

'That's because they're on the grass,' said Violet.

'Look at those fat greedy ducks. They're enormous. I guess people feed them every day.'

'Yeah, they do. Where've you been?'

'God knows. I got lost in France, but I'm here now so I'll try and make it up to you.'

Violet smiled. She had heard that so many times before!

CHAPTER 23

SHATTERED AT THE CHATEAU

After nearly two months of working at the Chateau Blanche, Linda felt happy but exhausted. She thought she had worked hard until she began this job! Fortunately, her understanding of the staff menus, rotas, and the vast expectations placed upon her had improved over the last few weeks. She now understood the importance of excellent wine, the family's reputation and the responsibility of running a first-class restaurant. She was sometimes amazed that Andre had considered her for the job when it was apparent that she had so much to learn, but he frequently said they needed someone who spoke English as many of their clientele came from the UK.

Linda was now excellent in the restaurant, and the office and Andre considered her an asset. His only regret was that his parents didn't share his opinion because they had wanted to employ someone French who had more experience with food. However, Linda had made some good suggestions about the decoration of the tables, which went down exceptionally well. She was able to use her creative skills to make subtle changes to the overall appearance of the restaurant, including the addition of flower arrangements. The days were long, and both Linda and Andre finished late at night. They occasionally found time in the morning to chat, or they sat drinking coffee together late into the night.

Linda was in awe of the Chateau's grandeur. It was the most incredible place she'd ever seen. Andre made sure that Linda took some hours off here and there to rest, so Linda often sat on a garden chair in the sun or walked around the vines, thinking about home. Linda loved her new job and being close to Andre, but over the past few weeks, it became evident that she missed her children, friends and salsa! Most of them had kept in touch via text, email and skype, but there was still an ache in her heart. It was vital to be committed to her work, so even if times got tough, she intended to stay. There was no choice when Adrian had made it categorically clear there would be no way back. Linda missed her walks to the brook with Peanut. It was sad not having a dog around, nor the spare time to walk one! Andre said now his parents were away, she could invite Ian to the Chateau, to make things easier, but Linda wasn't sure if he'd come. Ian had hardly kept in touch. He had taken the news of them parting badly, and Linda could sense a barrier between them. She hoped Fiona wouldn't distance herself, because it was very upsetting. Linda had explained to them both that they weren't in a relationship; Andre was a friend. He was not the reason she had left their father. But they found it hard to accept that their mother would travel such a distance for a job if there weren't something more when their mother hadn't worked for years!

It was early Sunday morning, and Linda was having a rare day off. She had already taken a shower in her petite bathroom. She was happy that her rooms were so charming and comfortable because she could relax. Her bedroom contained a four-poster bed, with floral drapes and a pair of matching full-length curtains hung from her window, framing a beautiful courtyard. The view from her window was amazing. There were numerous ornate hedges, which created different symmetrical patterns around a central fountain. Beyond that, she could see the vines which sloped towards the house in perfect rows. Today the sun had risen above the vines which had made them glow in anticipation of a fruitful harvest. Linda's phone suddenly buzzed as a voice message came in from Jade.

'Hi Linda, I miss you, babes. Yeah, I'd love to come and stay with you at the Chateau but could it be in a few weeks because I'm back at work now, and I'm busy! I've been having a great time with Brian. He's taking me to the beach at the weekend. No, I haven't seen Cameron, no one has. He's been looking after his child, something to do with his ex, who nearly died in hospital, bloody terrible. Only a few people have turned up at salsa, probably too hot! Oh, Sarah's been in her very short shorts! Ah yes, and George. He's started wearing tee shirts. He's lost tons of weight, but George is George lol! I hope you are having fun with Andre. He's so cute. Imagine having all that wine around you, you lucky thing! Are you behaving like me? I'm going to teach Kizomba to Brian so we can dance cheek to cheek!' I hope you are ok and Andre's parents have improved! Speak soon, Jade!'

Linda sighed. What a long message! Despite being in such a wonderful place, she almost felt envious of Jade going to salsa. It was brilliant that she was seeing Brian. They were now officially dating! She was slightly surprised but happy for her. Jade deserved someone who treated her well. Linda missed her infectious laughter, crude jokes and the occasional nudge in the ribs. It was beautiful at the Chateau, but things were different. Perhaps when she spoke French fluently, it would feel more comfortable. She would get there, but for now, the conversations were still confusing at times. Andre was happy she was around, and he often spoke about this, but he hadn't made any romantic moves apart from the occasional goodbye hug, or kiss on the cheek. Communication with him had been awkward when his parents were about because Andre didn't want to give the impression that he'd hired her for the wrong reasons, and she was grateful for that, but he then started to give her loud orders.

Linda hastily replied to Jade's voice message. She would look forward to seeing her whenever she could get a flight. Hopefully, it would be soon. Linda finished applying her clothes and makeup because Andre told her his parents were going away to Italy for a few weeks to visit friends so they would have the place to themselves and he planned to take her to Cannes today by car. Linda was thrilled by this and decided to wear her most expensive dress and jacket with newly acquired designer shades. She was still getting ready, when there was a knock at the door from Andre, it was only nine o'clock, and she was surprised. Andre explained that his parents had already left, and he was ready to go! Linda, couldn't wait to spend time with him alone so they could talk. The assistant manager who was a lovely cheerful French lady said that said they were quiet today and she would cover them both! Linda sighed, Cannes! She was, at last, going to see this beautiful place that had been her wish for many years and now all she could think about was dancing!

'Shall we not bother,' she said.

'What do you mean, not bother?' he replied in slightly broken English, looking shocked. 'Linda, today is my birthday. We must do something special. I've booked us dinner.'

'Yes, but I want to dance. I miss dancing so much. I can cope with being away from my friends, and I can manage without eating, but I simply can't manage without dance.'

'As today is my birthday, I will treat you to our very best champagne,' replied Andre, 'and yes, we shall dance.'

'Shall we dance?' asked Linda wistfully.

'Not here,' said Andre, 'in the ballroom'.

'What, I've been working here for a month, and you tell me the Chateau Blanche has a ballroom, does anyone use it?'

'No, not now. When I was a child, my parents had many parties. They invited people to taste the wine, but sadly that stopped years ago. I think it was the cost and it was difficult to take time out to entertain guests when they were so busy with the restaurant.'

'Did anyone dance?'

'Yes, but not salsa. We are the first to do that.'

'Can you find us some music?'

Andre poured the pink champagne into two cut glass champagne flutes, and they watched it bubble. Linda smiled at him. He was the most likeable and charming man she had ever had the pleasure to meet, and she found it incredible that he'd come into her life so unexpectedly. Andre had behaved like the perfect gentleman from the moment she met him. He had never tried to take advantage of her when they were alone, and Linda was grateful for that because she was still healing a broken heart from leaving home. Funnily, Linda had started to miss Adrian's old familiar drone, but nowhere near as much as the children and the dog. She sometimes thought she could hear Peanut walking up to her to lick her face. It felt as if he was still around her!

'Wait, I have some salsa music on my phone,' Andre said, as he laid it down on top of a heavy wooden table which seated at least twelve people! Linda marvelled at the beauty of the room. Long lined velvet curtains hung at each window. Linda counted at least ten windows, either side of the ballroom which filled it with light. What a shame that there were no longer any dances here. Perhaps in time, things would change, and there would be new energy, she thought glancing at the incredible chandeliers.

'You do realise that we are the only dancers at this dance?'

'No, we aren't alone. Many people are watching. People who have gone before,' answered Andre as he took her hand.

'What is this music, c'est tres familiar?' replied Linda as she noticed her French had improved.

'Ah, it's the salsa Latin version of an old song 'La Vie En Rose'.

'Alors je suis une rose?'

'No, you're not a rose. You are pink,' replied Andre. 'It means you see things in a good way, optimistically.'

'Well, the champagne is pink, and it's incredible. Quick pour me another before I forget how to dance. I am most certainly pink. I'm flushed.' she replied and started to giggle!

'Pink lady,' Andre repeated, laughing.

'English Rose,' she replied, as her very pink lips met his for their first proper embrace.

'You are so beautiful Linda. Can I marry you?'

'Andre I'm still married, but as it's your birthday, I want to give you a present.'

'What is this present?'

Linda leaned forward to whisper in his ear.

'You English. You are so, what is that word?'

'Naughty, yes I know,' said Linda smiling 'and we thrive on it!'

CHAPTER 24 - APOLOGISE?

It was Tuesday in mid-September, and Sarah had decided that the whole of her house could do with a damn good clean to brighten it up. If she had the time, she also wanted to paint. The worst place was the kitchen. It looked grimy. It was already magnolia, but it needed to be brighter.

Sarah had put on her rubber gloves and was making good progress. She had already cleaned the work surfaces, floor and windows which were dirtier than expected when she heard her mobile ring. She noticed it was Cameron and pulled off her soapy gloves. Sarah thought it would be easier to ignore him because he'd been a fling. Where could it go, after what happened between them in France? Sarah breathed and centred herself, then put her gloves back on and continued to clean. She had finished the inside of the oven, so there was just the hob, then she could stretch.

Sarah had yoga tomorrow. She wanted to work on something new to push her class. They were a great bunch who always turned up, and after weeks of consistency, they needed a challenge. Her mobile started to ring again. Whoever it was this time, they weren't going to give up. She had nearly finished so one last rinse, and she chucked her gloves in the sink to grab the phone.

'Hello,' she said, feeling annoyed at the interruption.

'Hi Sarah, it's Cameron.'

'Cameron, I don't wish to be rude, but I don't know why you are ringing me. I'm busy right now, and I don't have the time for this.'

'Why did you answer then?'

'I didn't realise it was you. I was cleaning my oven, so I just grabbed the phone.'

'I wondered if I could come back to yoga and maybe have a coffee somewhere. I want to explain about the earring because I know you were annoyed. I need to dance again. Looking after a child has been difficult. I love him to bits, but I miss my friends.'

'Why can't you explain now? We don't have to go for coffee. You can come to yoga if you want to, but I need people who are committed to every week. You know when my classes are because I gave you a schedule. Make sure you bring your mat though because I'm short.'

'Ok, no problem. I'm sorry I lied. I knew it was Jade's earring, but I found it on the ground outside the showers, nothing happened between us. What I like about you is that you are spiritual, and you know a lot about life. I could learn a lot from you.'

Sarah listened and didn't know what to say. She knew he was lying because she could hear it in his voice and even worse, was the false flattery.

'I like you because you are different, spiritual.' He knew how to flatter her! But he was trying to make amends despite the absence of integrity!

'Ok then, what have you learned?' she asked.

Cameron went quiet for ages, and Sarah thought he'd gone.

'I have learned a lot more about taking responsibility since I've been looking after Antonne and supporting his mother.'

'Oh, that's good. Yoga and meditation open you up to all sorts of things so you must be ready. You say you are taking responsibility, but that's just the beginning. You are welcome to come to my classes, but they are now yoga and meditation combined, I've changed the format slightly. It is now a six-week course, and you need to come to all six. Sarah was going to say sessions but thought better of it!

'So, you won't come on a date with me?' asked Cameron tentatively.

'No, I'm not ready for that Cameron, and neither are you. Not with me, anyway!'

'Do you think you're too good for me?' he asked.

'No, of course not, I don't want to go there with anyone right now. What happened in France was a one-off. I don't see it as anything else, but I need to focus on myself now and stay in a good place.'

'The good place, yeah, I've watched that on Netflix!''

'I'm sorry I've got to go now. I start back next week if you want to come,' Sarah replied, completely ignoring his poor joke. The man was incorrigible, and she didn't need it.

Cameron put on the kettle and grabbed two mugs off the mug tree. He usually made tea for Violet when she was busy with Antonne. Thankfully it was Saturday, and they had both been able to have a little longer to rest this morning. They had a good friendship between them now. He was aware that Violet wanted more, but he couldn't give it. He didn't feel that way about her. The attraction between them had long gone, but he did care.

Violet walked into the kitchen at the sound of the kettle.

'Shall I make us a fry up?' she asked.

'No thanks, I don't eat bacon. I've gone vegan.' Cameron replied.

'Gone vegan? Are you fucking joking? What's the matter with you? Who were you talking to for so long?'

'Who was I talking to?' We are back there again, aren't we? I do care about you, but this is never going to work Babes. I'm sorry, Violet, but I'm not your man. I respect you because you are the mother of my child, but we don't want the same things. I don't want to stay here if you're going to ask me questions persistently.

'What's wrong with questions?' replied Violet, who was on the verge of tears. She had hoped that Cameron would come around. She loved him, and it felt right them being together.

'I think I better move back to my flat. I'm still paying for it, and it's sitting there empty. You are a lot better now. You can manage it. I'll still come and fix things up for you. I'll fix the cupboards today. There are a couple that if left any longer, will fall off their hinges,' he said a little more gently.

'Don't go, Cameron. I need you here.'

'You don't need me, Violet. You were fine on your own until you got sick. Go and do that Degree or something, I will pop over and look after Antonne. Do it for you.'

Violet walked out of the kitchen and sat down on the sofa with her tea. Antonne was watching a cartoon on TV. She didn't like him watching television because he was too young, but he was fascinated. Her heart was breaking. Why couldn't Cameron see what they had? Who was he chasing now, some woman from dancing? What, was all this vegan stuff? He'd be back. He hadn't grown up yet not entirely, and she would be waiting because she was right for him in so many ways. Some woman may hold his interest now, but he wouldn't stay with her. He never did. He was a restless soul who had to keep moving on. She wasn't sure why. Maybe he needed more love as a child. Then he would have learned how to give love. It was always about the chase, the excitement, the thrill. Violet sometimes wondered if Cameron had other children. If he did, she would never know because his head was full of neat little boxes. Getting Cameron to reveal his deeper feelings was arduous, and she'd given that up a long time ago.

Violet sighed and abruptly turned off the television which made Antonne scream. She then heard Cameron shut the front door. She had no idea where he was going or if he'd be back!

CHAPTER 25

HARRIETT & EMILY

'It's on Friday? Of course, I will come, but don't you think it's about time you told your parents, after all, we can't keep pretending forever!'

'No, not yet, I want to be sure everything is ok, and that I want to keep it.'

'We've talked about this and decided yes, we do. It was unplanned, but I'm happy to help you look after your child. I'm excited this baby will be part of our family.

'I'm terrified. I'm not sure I want this at all. I know I can't go back, but it's going to get awkward, and there will be questions.'

'He doesn't know, does he?' asked Emily.

'No, of course not. I'm sure he doesn't have a clue because it was a one-off when he was drunk. He was so miserable about that Sarah woman.

I'm not sure why he even called. I think he wanted to get a few things off his chest. I felt kind of sorry for him because his ex-partner was in the hospital, and he said something about how he had to get back to look after his child.'

'What, he has a child already?'

'Yes, and he doesn't want to look after him either! I think it's a boy, so there is no way I'm telling him about this!'

'What about everyone else, the rest of the salsa lot?'

'I haven't been to Salsa since France, so it's not a problem.'

'What time is the scan? I will be there, but I will have to get an early train from London. I can stay at the weekend so we can tell your parents together! I will have to go back Sunday morning or the evening though because I have so much work on!'

'That's fine. It won't be long until we are together permanently. After the scan, it will be easier to tell Mum and Dad because I will know more. I've worked out that I'm around twelve weeks, but it will be good to have it confirmed,' Harriett explained anxiously. She dreaded telling her parents. They despaired of her working as a Nanny when they had scrimped to send her to a posh boarding school. It hadn't been easy for them, and now she had to tell them this! They didn't even know she was gay, let alone pregnant. What would she say to them? I got pregnant with a man when we were drunk. By the way, I'm a lesbian and, this is my partner! Harriett kept imagining her baby was kicking, although she knew it was way too early because right now the baby would be a tiny thing. Even though the situation was utterly crazy, she had a sense of pride about her condition, which made her realise that on one level, she had wanted it to happen.

Harriett wondered what they would call the baby? Perhaps something different, or named after one of her grandparents, something traditional? She didn't know at what stage the hospital could tell the sex? She wasn't sure about that either. Life was about surprises, and some of them had to be good! Not everything was predictable. Surprises could also bring joy. That was what irritated her about her parents. They had all these ideas, but they were their ideas, not hers. She hadn't made any promises to fulfil their dreams. They had to do that themselves.

Harriett loved Emily, the divorcee she worked for with two young children. It was a complete surprise when this relationship started because she was unsure of her sexuality. But over the last few months, Harriett became increasingly attracted to Emily. The lady was a sweet angel, and it wasn't until recently that Emily revealed she too was gay and explained to Harriett the reasons why her marriage broke up. They talked for hours after the children had gone to bed and began to form a strong friendship. Emily often worked late, and Harriett would prepare a meal for the children and another dinner for them which was exhausting, but she loved it. Harriett couldn't wait to move into the house permanently not as an employee but as partners. In London, she could be herself, which was a huge relief. She wished the incident had never happened with Cameron, but despite her intense feelings for Emily, Cameron felt like a kindred spirit. They had a lot in common, yoga, dance, attitude, and they shared the same sense of humour.

Harriett was relieved that Emily was attending the scan because she was scared there could be something wrong. Were all young mothers like this, or was it just her? If everything went to plan, they were going to tell her parents about the baby before Emily returned to London. Harriett felt guilty about not saying anything to Cameron, but she hadn't seen him for three months, and he would never want to be a live-in Dad. Emily's children would be thrilled about a baby coming into the household, and they wouldn't be worried about how it came about. The little girl who was now two was continually asking her Mum for a baby brother or sister. It would be a dream come true for the children.

It was early Friday morning, and Harriett went to pick Emily up from the station. She patiently waited in her car for Emily's train. It would be in soon because it was the next train to arrive from London. She turned on her phone and started to listen to some salsa tracks. She missed salsa. But it didn't feel the right time to dance, being three months pregnant! She would ask the Doctor about that at her appointment today. Surely a little salsa wouldn't cause harm thought Harriett as her feet started to move to the music!

Emily arrived. She looked immaculate in a gorgeous short floaty skirt and cream matching jacket. She'd come straight from her office.

'God, it was such a rush but please don't worry darling, I'm not complaining. You're worth it. Are you ready to go? Let's go and meet this little bundle of joy. It's so exciting. I bet as soon as you see our baby on the screen, you'll cry. I did,' said Emily enthusiastically.

'I'm sorry. Do you wish it was you?' asked Harriett.

'No, of course not. I've already been through this twice remember, and I'm perfectly happy with Christopher and Jenny. I'm excited for you, though. It will be fantastic to have a new addition to our family.

Harriett and Emily pulled up in the hospital car park and started to walk towards the outpatients.

'Do you know the way, Harriett?' asked Emily. 'We are a little on the late side.'

'No, I thought you did! Where's that piece of paper with a map to the maternity unit?'

'I don't know. I assumed as it was your appointment, you would have the map. Look, let's not make a fuss about it. We can go to the main reception and ask. We'll be fine. I expect the hospital's use to people arriving late, being maternity!'

Harriett felt slightly annoyed. She knew she had given Emily the map, and now it had disappeared. If she caught the earlier train, it would have been better. Now they had to rush!

'The Maternity Block is straight ahead. Turn left, then go past the stairs, turn right and take the lift. Have you got that?' asked the young Receptionist, who Harriett thought looked fifteen.

'No, but I have. I'm good with the layout of buildings,' answered Emily a little sarcastically.

They walked quickly along the corridors. Then Emily noticed the signs to various departments. It appeared Maternity was on the top floor. As they approached the lift, they saw a couple standing inside with a young child, and to Harriett's horror, she realised it was Cameron.

'Let's go, we can take the stairs,' she whispered to Emily as she turned away.

'Harriett, what the fuck is the matter with you? It's on the 9th floor. We need to take the lift, or we won't get there on time!'

'No, we...'

Suddenly there was a voice coming from inside the lift and Harriett noticed that Cameron was standing there holding the button, waiting for them to enter.

'Hey, Harriett, what are you doing here?' he asked.

'I was going to ask you the same thing?' she replied as she tried to hide her tiny bump.'

'Oh, I brought Violet in for a check-up because she had an operation a few months ago and she's been getting a bit of pain. They want to check that everything is ok. I didn't see you at dancing, so I assumed you were in London?'

'I'm here for the weekend. Anyway, Cameron, this is Emily, my partner.'

'Nice to meet you. Do you dance Emily?' Cameron was taking his time to select the floors, and the lift was at a standstill!

'No, but I'd love to. It sounds great fun.' replied Emily.

'Are you visiting someone?' continued Cameron as the lift began to move.

'Yes, we're going to visit a friend in maternity, on the top floor,' explained Emily.

Cameron and Violet waved goodbye, and Violet took Antonne's hand to help him out of the lift.

'Wow, his son looks sweet, although the woman didn't look happy,' whispered Harriett.

'Yeah, we need to hurry now,' Emily replied, or we won't make it in time.

'You didn't have to say we were going to maternity Emily! I don't want him to find out.'

'Even if he noticed your microscopic bump, he doesn't know it's his, does he?' replied Emily, sounding indifferent to the whole thing.

Ten minutes later and Harriett sat propped up with pillows with Emily by her side. They were both looking at the screen while a young radiologist ran the transducer over Harriett's stomach.

'That jelly feels cold,' exclaimed Harriett. 'Wow, look at the screen. You can make out the shape of our baby.'

'Oh my God, that's incredible,' replied Emily with tears streaming down her face.

'Yes, there you are. Your baby is healthy, with a strong heartbeat. Congratulations, you must be excited. Oh, hang on a minute, I may be wrong, but I think I can see two heartbeats. Let me call the Dr in to check, but I'm reasonably sure.

The young radiologist quickly returned with the Doctor, who asked Harriett how she was feeling before looking at the screen.

'Yes, well done. There are two heartbeats. Look, you can see them both.'

Emily and Harriett looked at the heartbeats in amazement!

Harriett didn't know what to say. She was in complete shock. It had never occurred to her that this could happen. There were no twins in her family!

'What about the father? Are there twins in his family?' asked the Doctor.

'I don't know,' answered Harriett.

'The father doesn't know,' replied Emily.

'Is that your decision Harriett? Twins can be difficult. Looking after them is extremely hard.'

'That's ok. I have Emily to help me. She's my partner.'

'Oh, I see. Well, you will be looking after one each, and there won't be much time for anything else. Your life will be giving feeds changing nappies and occasionally taking them out!'

'Yes, I'm sure she'll be fine. She's used to hard work. She's a Designer.'

Harriett turned to look at Emily, but she'd gone. She then noticed her talking on her mobile.

'A designer can design an incredible nursery, I suppose but please think about what I said Harriett, I can't make you do anything, but you will need all the help you can get.'

'I know. I'm going to tell my parents today.'

'That's an excellent idea,' replied the Doctor

Emily came and sat at the side of the bed. 'I've told the children, and they are very excited. We'll make a fabulous little family.'

'Wow, you have told them already. I'm not sure how I feel about the children knowing before my parents, but I guess they will need to know eventually. Let's go and get a coffee and work out what we're going to say to Mum and

Dad. I may as well tell them the truth. They won't be happy, but at least they will know my babies are going to be loved by the two of us and they'll have a brother and sister.'

Harriett felt strange. She could hear the words as she spoke, but none of it felt real, and at the back of her mind, she wondered if Emily would stick by her. It was going to be hard, and it would completely change both their lives. For the first time, she wondered if Cameron had a right to know. She was giving birth to his children! She had wanted to keep it a secret, so he didn't have any rights which could prove messy and complicated, but now she felt differently.

Was Emily a little controlling? Imagine her telling her children before she had the chance to talk to her parents. Was she going to keep telling everyone her business before she was ready? They were her babies! She still couldn't take it in. It was incredible! One hurdle at a time she thought as they left the hospital and the first would be her Mum and Dad!

CHAPTER 26

YOGA

It was a Monday morning in September, and Sarah had already laid out her yoga mats. She closed her eyes and began to centre her energy by focusing on her breath. Meditation always helped her to stay balanced and grounded. The class had enjoyed the addition of a short meditation, where they went on a journey. They often had a five to ten-minute discussion about what they felt afterwards, which often proved interesting.

To Sarah's surprise, Cameron arrived early and sat down on his mat, wearing a pair of black joggers and tee shirt. Sarah thought he looked peaceful and a little gorgeous! There were now twelve regular pupils, and Sarah was pleased with the group's commitment. She started by asking them to relax their bodies and focus on the breath. She always kept aware of what was happening for everyone, and after ten minutes, she said 'ok then, wiggle your fingers and toes and come back into the room.' Today, Cameron was the last to open his eyes.

'Ok then, I hope that helped. All of you look very relaxed today, which is wonderful. Would anyone like to tell the group how you felt?' asked Sarah

'Yes, I would,' answered Cameron.

Sarah was worried about what he would say, but as Cameron had recently joined her class and had paid for six sessions, she had to allow him to speak.

'I saw a little boy. He was running on a big empty beach. He was alone. The boy felt frightened. He wanted to cry and scream where was everyone, but instead, he sat down on the beach and looked at the sea. As he put his hand down on the sand, he felt a giant shell which he held to his ear. He heard the sea inside it, but there was also a voice which said, follow the footsteps in the sand. The boy stood up and saw footsteps straight in front of him. They looked big, strong and familiar, so he took off his socks and shoes to place his feet in them. As he walked, he began to feel comfortable in them and the journey they took. He soon realised they were his own! His pace quickened, and he grew in confidence. The footprints led him back to where he started. He looked down at himself and saw that he had grown into a man. He turned and waved at the little boy who was still sitting on the beach. The boy was busy making a sandcastle, creating his dreams. He had covered the sandcastle with many beautiful shells which he could put to his ear so he would never be lonely or frightened. He knew he would grow into a confident man.

'Do you like sandcastles Cameron?' asked Sarah, who found the story he had shared with the group astounding.

'Yes, I do, but I forgot how to build them, so I gave up on my dreams.'

'Yes, following our dreams is essential. We all have constant distractions, and we can easily forget. Would anyone else like to share their experience?' said Sarah, addressing the class.

Sarah realised that the rest of the group had gone very quiet because they had been listening to Cameron's fascinating story.

'I forgot my dreams, too,' answered a man from the back of the hall.

'I was so wrapped up in myself that I lost my house, wife and children. Everything important to me had gone. I used to skim stones, swim in rivers, dance, and run on the beach. I embraced everything. Then I stopped caring. Everyone was a nuisance; I could only see me.'

I'm sorry about that. I hope things have improved since then?' asked Cameron.

'Yeah, I woke up to who I am. Yoga and meditation helped. I've been going to yoga for over twenty years now and have a wonderful wife who loves and supports me,' he said, smiling at Jane, his partner, who always sat next to him in the class.

Sarah smiled. The couple had been on her last course. They had been going to yoga together for many years.

'Thank you,' said Sarah. She wondered if she was going to have time for the yoga part of the class! Perhaps it was better to keep the meditation separate after all!

'I saw a dancing fairy, and I could suddenly dance,' explained a young lady in the middle row. She appeared overweight, and Sarah noticed that she was uncomfortable with her body.

'I told the fairy I always wanted to dance, but my mother said I was too fat and laughed at me. I was large at school. I've always been clumsy. The fairy said I was beautiful and graceful, and I needed to forget labels. She made me write a new one and tie it on myself. I tried to look at the words, but they were difficult to read because the letters were in gold swirly writing. As I moved closer to read it, I suddenly saw myself swirling around until I was spinning. I had dance shoes on my feet, and I was counting.'

'Salsa,' shouted Cameron, rather abruptly, 'I can teach you that!'

'Salsa,' replied Sarah. 'Well, maybe we can teach you together. We could start a class, and call it something like believing in dance,' said Sarah, smiling.

'Belief in you,' Cameron replied. 'I like that. We can make it happen,' continued Cameron.

'We have to move on to the stretches now. The time has gone so fast. We've only twenty minutes left!' Sarah explained as she tried to motivate the class.

'After the stretches, Cameron walked over to Sarah and said 'I think us starting a dance class together is a brilliant idea. That's if you're serious?'

'I'm always serious Cameron, but dance lightens me, so does yoga. Did you enjoy the class? Thank you for sharing your experience. It was beneficial for everyone. You do realise that little boy was your inner child, a part of you?'

'I know, I realised that as I was talking. I love the beach, and I've always dreamed about making a massive sandcastle with a moat!'

'Would you like to finish one?' asked Sarah.

'Yes, I would.'

'Well let's go for a coffee and talk about our new dance class before the sea comes in. We may as well enjoy it while we can.'

'So, you're over the earring. I'm forgiven?'

'We all have a past Cameron, including me. Let's focus on building something new together and see where it takes us.'

'That will be fun,' he replied.

'Where would you like to go for coffee?' asked Sarah.

'Felixstowe,' where we can look at the sea and dance on the sand. It isn't the Riviera, I know, but it will be fun,' he said, enthusiastically.

'Fun, I'm still learning about that, but dance has taught me so much,' she said, smiling.

'I think you are beautiful,' said Cameron as he leaned forward to kiss her.

'Let's go,' she said boldly.

'Yes, let's go. Maybe we can take Antonne with us next time. He loves the beach.'

'We'll see. Let's go one step at a time. But don't tread on my toes again, or you'll be in big trouble,' Sarah warned.

'I wouldn't dare!' he said then laughed!

'Is that your mobile?' asked Sarah.

'Yes, I thought it was off, sorry, it could have disturbed the class. I'll turn it off. Whoever's calling can wait,' replied Cameron, not pausing to look.

'Have you got some music,' asked Sarah.

'Yes, on my phone, but I'm leaving that off,' he replied.

'How do you keep the music playing?'

'You dance' he said.

The beach was stony, but they managed to find a flat area where the tide had gone out, to dance. Sarah and Cameron practised some new steps that Cameron introduced, which were a combination of both Cuban and Crossbody. Sarah found dancing the two types of salsa together exciting, and she was keen to learn. After about an hour they walked up the beach and looked at the waves. The sea was now rough, and they both felt chilly.

'I've got to head back now Cameron. I'm having dinner with my parents tonight, and I don't want to be late, but I've had a fantastic time. I'm sorry we didn't build a sandcastle, but like you say we can do that another time.'

'Yes, it is getting a little chilly now, let's head back.'

As Sarah headed off, Cameron decided to buy a portion of chips from a nearby kiosk and eat them while watching the sea from his car. He felt happy, which was something he hadn't felt for years. It would be a challenge to keep Sarah interested because she was an articulate woman who knew what she wanted. He had already blown it once, but he wanted to keep trying. He liked Sarah, and he was excited about their plan to start a dance class.

When he finished his chips, he wiped his hands on the wrapper, screwed up the paper and placed it inside his car door because it was far too blowy to go out and search for a bin! As he turned his ignition key to drive away, he suddenly realised that his hat was missing. He guessed it must have blown off while they danced on the beach! Cameron quickly jumped out of his car, dumped the chip wrapper in a bin and headed towards the sandy part of the beach where they had danced. The tide had come in about six feet, and his hat was now in the water. It occurred to him to leave it because the sea had turned rough and the hat looked soggy. But it was his favourite, and he always wore it when he danced!

Cameron crouched down and stretched forward to reach his hat. He had to focus on his balance because he didn't want to fall into the sea. The beach looked utterly deserted. As his hand grabbed it, he suddenly heard a voice that sounded like Linda. 'Don't forget your hat,' she said. He smiled, remembering the times she had told him that as he left her home. Cameron quickly shook the water out of the hat and hurried back to his car to drive home. As he sat down, he accidentally sat on his phone in his rear pocket. He quickly removed it to make sure it was in one piece! To his relief, the screen was intact, but there were two missed calls and a text. It was quite a drive home, and he wanted to get going, but as the text message was from Jade, he decided to open it.

'Hi Cameron, this is urgent. Please ring me back because something terrible has happened. The French Police found Linda dead on the beach early this morning. They said that she must have gone for an early morning swim, after an all-night party. They're not sure whether it was an accident or suicide, but she'd been drinking. Jade

Cameron read the message twice. Was Jade saying Linda was dead? They must have made a mistake. The last time he'd heard about her, she was having a ball with this French guy, Andre! He sat for a few moments in complete shock. He then picked up his wet hat and placed it on his head. It was strange that he'd heard Linda's voice down by the sea and he looked about him to make sure she wasn't on the beach waiting.

The two missed calls were from numbers he didn't recognise. Could one have been France? As Cameron started up his engine, a tear trickled down his cheek, and for the first time, he realised that he loved her.

Printed in Great Britain
by Amazon

61224880R00138